The Land of Green Ginger

NOEL LANGLEY

ILLUSTRATED BY EDWARD ARDIZZONE

FABER & FABER

First published as *The Tale of the Land of Green Ginger* in 1937
This version first published in 1966
This edition first published in 2015
Faber & Faber Limited
Bloomsbury House, 74–77 Great Russell Street
London, WC1B 3DA

A CIP record for this book is available from the British Library

Designed and typeset by Crow Books
Printed and bound by CPI Group (UK) Ltd, Croydon, CR0 4YY

ISBN 978–0–571–32134–6

FSC
www.fsc.org
MIX
Paper from
responsible sources
FSC® C101712

4 6 8 10 9 7 5 3 1

"*The Land of Green Ginger* is that unlikeliest of things, a **funny** book for children that is, actually, funny; a **glorious magical adventure** laced with a **dry humour**, as if Evelyn Waugh had secretly written a panto. We follow Aladdin's son, Abu Ali, on his quest to untransform a wizard who has been changed into a button-nosed tortoise, assisted by a relatively useless Genie, a mouse, and Omar Khayyam, while being frustrated at every step by the evil princes Tintac Ping Foo and Rubdub Ben Thud. It is **smart and fun from beginning to end**. Also it has a half chapter, which most books don't."

Neil Gaiman

FABER & FABER
has published children's books since 1929. Some of our very first publications included *Old Possum's Book of Practical Cats* by T. S. Eliot, starring the now world-famous Macavity, and *The Iron Man* by Ted Hughes. Our catalogue at the time said that 'it is by reading such books that children learn the difference between the shoddy and the genuine'. We still believe in the power of reading to transform children's lives.

Contents

Chapter the First

*Which Explains How, Why, When, and Where There Was
Ever Any Problem in the First Place*

May fortune preserve you, Gentle Reader. May your days be filled with constant joys, and may my story please you, for it has no other purpose.

And now, if you are ready to begin, I bring you a tale of heroes and villains, just as in life; birds and beasts, just as in zoos; mysteries and magic, just as in daydreams; and the wonderful wanderings of an enchanted land which was never in the same place twice.

As long ago as long ago, and as long ago again as that, the city of Peking in the ancient land of China rang with jubilation and rejoicing; for a son and heir had been born to the Emperor Aladdin and the Empress Bedr-el-Budur; the lily whose glad renown I have no need to gild.

1

To commemorate the auspicious occasion, the Emperor Aladdin had announced a firework display in the palace park, and ordered elegant paper flags, cut in the shapes of golden birds and fishes, to be given to the people of Peking. When these were waved in every available inch of the crowded street, the sight was quite enchanting.

On a more serious note, the Grand Vizier summoned a special meeting of state in the White Lacquer Room of the Imperial Palace.

You may judge for yourself the importance of this meeting, when I tell you that His Gracious Majesty the Emperor Aladdin presided over it himself. Others present included the Lord Chamberlain; the Prime Minister; two senior generals from the Palace Guard; the Master of the Horse; the Mistress of the Robes; and an unidentified friend of the Master of the Horse.

The Grand Vizier himself, having forgotten that he had called the special meeting, had gone to watch the fireworks display in the palace park instead; but, alas, though the display had been advertised to commence promptly at one hour after sunset, hitches

and vexations had arisen, and as yet the park was dark and silent.

He then remembered the special meeting, and arrived not only last, but a little out of breath from slipping on a mat in the ante-room.

Regaining his aplomb, he beat importantly on a dragon gong with an ivory wand, and everyone present nodded encouragingly to indicate their willingness to listen attentively to whatever he was going to say.

'Your Majesty!' began the Grand Vizier imposingly. 'Also Lords and Ladies of the Imperial Court! Also the friend of the Master of the Horse. We are met here this evening to give formal voice to our humble and unworthy joy at the birth of a son and heir to our Celestial Emperor of all the Chinas –'

Here everyone present rose dutifully and bowed to the Emperor Aladdin, and seated themselves again.

'– and to offer our ridiculous and ineffectual assistance in deciding what name or names shall be given to the said son and heir of our Celestial Emperor of all the Chinas –'

Here everyone present rose and bowed to the Emperor Aladdin and seated themselves again; causing the Emperor Aladdin to address them personally.

'Henceforth,' he said considerately, 'you may dispense with the ceremony of rising and bowing at the mention of my name, or we'll never finish this special meeting, and I am naturally anxious not to miss the fireworks which, after all, I paid for. You may proceed, Grand Vizier.'

4

'Thank you, Your Majesty,' said the Grand Vizier. 'To proceed,' he proceeded, 'I cannot stress the importance of the solemn duty which is ours. It is a duty, I think I may safely say, which the whole of China looks to us to bear honourably, shoulder to shoulder, one for all and all for one, and long live the Emperor of all the Chinas –'

Whereupon everyone present rose and bowed to the Emperor Aladdin, and then remembered that he had specifically asked them not to, and seated themselves hurriedly, feeling slightly foolish.

'I said I could not stress the importance of the solemn duty which is ours,' continued the Grand Vizier, 'and it's quite true. I can't. But that's life. You have each been given,' he said, 'a piece of paper and a pencil –'

The Lord Chamberlain raised his hand.

'I beg your pardon,' he said imposingly, 'but by some pardonable error I have been given no pencil.'

'You have *each* been given,' said the Grand Vizier in a sharper voice, 'a piece of paper and a pencil. On the piece of paper, with the pencil, you will write –'

'No pencil,' said the Lord Chamberlain clearly and distinctly.

'Order, order,' murmured the Master of the Horse reproachfully.

'*On* the piece of paper, *with* the pencil,' said the Grand Vizier very sharply indeed, 'you will write five names for the heir apparent to the throne, all of which must be suitable, dignified, and poetic. The papers will then be collected and handed to the Emperor, who will decide which name he likes best. A word of caution,' he added gravely. 'I depend on you not to peep at each other's pieces of paper. Anyone found doing this will have his piece of paper torn up, and will not be allowed to watch the fireworks.

'The winner will be awarded the Empress's clockwork nightingale, which can sing three songs flawlessly, once a few minor repairs have been made. The consolation prize is a ride once around the palace on an elephant.'

'No pencil,' said the Lord Chamberlain, pathetic now.

The Master of the Horse, who was kinder than

some I could mention, broke his pencil in two and gave the Lord Chamberlain the blunt half, and silence fell as everybody present began to think of five suitable, dignified, and poetic names.

Everybody present sat, and they thought, and they thought very hard, frowning now at the floor, and now at the ceiling, and occasionally at the Emperor Aladdin, though not intentionally; but no one seemed able to think of any names at all, except useless ones like *Tea-Pot* and *Bird's Nest Soup*.

Time went by, and the Emperor Aladdin began peering over his shoulder at the window, in case the fireworks started without him; and the special

meeting began to feel desperate at not being able to think of five suitable, dignified, and poetic names.

At last the silence was broken by the Lord Chamberlain, who suddenly said: '*Ah!*' very excitedly and sucked his pencil and got his piece of paper ready, and everyone present looked at him with envy, and thought to themselves how much they had always loathed the Lord Chamberlain.

The moment he put his pencil to the piece of paper, however, the name he had thought of vanished into thin air; but, as everyone was looking at him, and he had to write *something,* he wrote 'Lord Chamberlain' in curly capitals: hoping to cross it out later, unobserved.

Another silence fell, and the Master of the Horse rose and made his cushion more comfortable and seated himself again; but even so, the only names he could think of were the names of horses, which were almost as unsuitable as *Tea-Pot* and *Bird's Nest Soup.*

From where the Emperor Aladdin sat on the throne, he could see all the pieces of paper, and the Lord Chamberlain's was the only one with any

8

words on it (and those were crossed out); so at last his impatience got the better of him, and he rose and said with frigid politeness:

'If it will not disturb your train of thought, I shall excuse myself and retire to the balcony, as I think I heard a bang.'

Everyone present rose and bowed while he departed for the balcony, and then reseated themselves, and the Lord Chamberlain rather forlornly wrote 'Bang' on his piece of paper, then thought better of it, and drew little faces down the side instead, to help him concentrate.

Out on the balcony, the Emperor Aladdin discovered that the hitches and vexations were still delaying the fireworks, and he was about to return to the special meeting, when the Queen Mother, the Honourable Widow Twankey, found him.

'Ah, *there* you are!' she cried very loudly, seizing him by the sleeve. 'My pearl-encrusted snuffbox, Aladdin! That *son* of yours! My sapphire tiara! What a child!'

'There's no use to bellow, mamma,' Aladdin told

Button-Nosed Tortoise

her kindly, trying to pull his sleeve free. 'We all *know* how happy you are about it –'

'Happy?' echoed the Widow Twankey, unamused. '*Happy?* When your son has just called me, *me*, the Queen Mother, a button-nosed tortoise?'

'Tut! Calm yourself, mamma,' Aladdin soothed her. 'A day-old baby doesn't talk!'

'I *know* it doesn't!' replied the Widow Twankey loudly. 'And I know how old my grandson is, to the minute; but he *still* called me a button-nosed tortoise! So don't just *stand* there, Aladdin! *Do* something!'

The Emperor controlled an impulse to say, 'Do

what?' or 'Such as?', and proceeded to the Yellow Lacquer Nurseries. There he found his son and heir gazing at his foot, which he held near his nose with both hands.

He bent over the cradle and waved his fingers.

'Hootchie-cootchie, my itsywitsy!' said the Emperor Aladdin indulgently. 'Did his grandma say de Emperor's own handsome itty melon-flower could talk? Tum on den, talk to oo papa!'

The son and heir lowered his foot and gazed up at the Emperor Aladdin attentively for a moment.

'Certainly!' he replied good-naturedly. 'Hootchie-cootchie to you, too! Twice.'

'Dere's a clever itty boo!' said the Emperor Aladdin, much gratified, and then sat down quickly on a nearby chair and opened and shut his mouth in a very dazed manner.

'*Now* do you believe me?' asked the Widow Twankey with gloomy satisfaction.

The Emperor Aladdin rallied himself, and gazed at his son and heir with as much dignity as he could muster.

'I understand you called the Queen Mother a button-nosed tortoise?' he inquired.

'That's not quite true,' replied his son and heir politely. 'I only said she had a face like one.'

'He only said you had a face like one, mamma,' Aladdin explained weakly.

'And what right had he to say even that?' demanded the Widow Twankey indignantly. 'Even if there *were* such a thing as a button-nosed tortoise; *he* hasn't seen one!'

'True,' agreed the son and heir, 'but I'd know one if I *did* see one!'

'How?' the Widow Twankey challenged him.

'It'd look like you,' said the son and heir simply.

'Aladdin! I refuse to be insulted! Do something!' ordered the Widow Twankey angrily.

The Emperor Aladdin looked twice as helpless as he had before.

'Do what?' he asked. 'Such as? I'm completely at a loss! Out of all the thousands and *thousands* of expectant fathers in Peking, why did this have to happen to me?'

'Maybe the stork brought me to the wrong palace?' suggested his son and heir apologetically.

'I didn't mean to sound unfatherly,' the Emperor Aladdin floundered kind-heartedly. 'It's just that – it's simply that – what I mean is,' he explained, 'it doesn't *happen*! It's not *possible*! You can't talk at your age! That's all there is to it!'

'Ah, I begin to grasp the problem!' said the son and heir, looking suitably pensive. 'It clearly calls for careful thinking on everybody's part.'

'It's obviously an enchantment, or a wicked spell, or both, or worse!' declared the Widow Twankey darkly. 'My ormolu ear-rings! I know what's happened, Aladdin! Your wicked uncle Abanazar is back in town!'

'No, mamma,' said the Emperor Aladdin. 'Our spies, who are everywhere, would have informed us. He's *miles* away in Persia, where we banished him.'

'Which side of the family is wicked uncle Abanazar?' asked the son and heir, intrigued. 'And does *he* have a face like a button-nosed tortoise, too?'

'That'll be enough from you!' the Widow Twankey

warned him, growing red. 'I can stand just so much!'

'The wisest move that *I* can think of,' said the Emperor Aladdin, 'is to ask Abdul *his* opinion.'

'What? Abdul? Never!' cried the Widow Twankey in alarm. 'When you gave him his freedom, you promised him you never would rub that lamp again!'

'Who is Abdul?' asked the son and heir, with cordial interest. 'Another member of the family?'

'No. He's the slave of the lamp,' said the Emperor Aladdin. 'But you wouldn't know about the lamp. When I was but a boy, my wicked uncle Abanazar sent me down into a cave to find it, and then he sealed me up there. In my alarm, I chanced to rub the lamp by accident, and Abdul appeared and told me I had but to command and he would obey. Well, to cut a long story short, I took him at his word, and that, my child, was how I met your mother. While it's perfectly true that I promised him I wouldn't use the lamp again, once I gave him his freedom; I'm sure he'll understand that, faced with an emergency such as this, I really had no other choice!'

He clapped his hands for a Lady-in-Waiting who

was conveniently listening just outside the door.

'Kindly bring the lamp,' he ordered her rather grandly, being nervous, 'and be careful not to let it rub against anything on the way.'

'I'll be *sure* not to!' said the Lady-in-Waiting with heart-felt sincerity.

'Of course, it may not even work any more,' he said as the Lady-in-Waiting departed, wearing her uneasiest expression, 'but, if anyone'll know what to do, Abdul will! Good old Abdul!' he added in a wavery attempt to sound confident and optimistic.

'Never say I didn't warn you!' said the Widow Twankey ominously. 'If he takes it the wrong way, and creates an ugly scene, I shall *not* be party to it!'

The Lady-in-Waiting came back with the lamp at arm's length on a cushion, and as soon as the Emperor Aladdin took it, she disappeared so fast it hardly seemed possible.

The Emperor Aladdin held up the lamp cautiously between his finger and thumb.

'Well, well, well,' he said slowly, looking at it from one end and then the other and, finally, sideways.

'And to think I once handled it as casually as tap your top-knot!'

'Well, *rub* the thing if you're going to!' snapped the Widow Twankey irritably. 'Don't just sit there twiddling it! Consider my nerves!'

'Very well,' said Aladdin. 'Here we go; ready or not!'

'I *still* hope he won't come; but if he does, tell me when he's gone! I'm not going to look!' announced the Widow Twankey, putting her fingers in her ears and screwing her eyes tight shut. She looked so absurd that the son and heir was unable to repress a giggle.

The Emperor Aladdin glanced over at him in reproach.

'I don't think you ought to look, either,' he advised him gravely. 'Abdul's hardly what you'd call handsome!'

'Why, the uglier the better!' said his son and heir cheerfully, leaning over the end of his cot. 'Hurry up and rub the lamp, papa, unless you're scared!'

The Emperor Aladdin stiffened.

'For your particular information, I am not scared in the slightest!' he said haughtily.

The Widow Twankey opened one eye.

'You don't mean you haven't rubbed it *yet*?' she demanded indignantly.

'More haste, less speed,' said the Emperor Aladdin, still ruffled. 'There's such a thing as correct procedure!'

'Here! Let *me* do it!' said the Widow Twankey impatiently, and snatched the lamp out of the Emperor's hands. 'Even if it's only to prove that he'll refuse to answer!'

She had no sooner brushed the lamp with her sleeve, however, when a loud clap of thunder resounded through the room. The Widow Twankey gave a shrill wail, flung the lamp in the air, dug her fingers back into her ears, and squeezed her eyes twice as tightly shut as before.

The Emperor Aladdin and his son and heir were too occupied to notice. They were watching the floor, which was slowly cracking open down the middle.

As the thunder died away, a large cloud of green

smoke rose up through the crack in the floor, and hovered imposingly in the middle of the room.

Then the floor closed together, leaving no sign of the crack, and slowly and impressively, Abdul's huge green saucer-eyes began to glow through the cloud like lamps.

His big bulbous nose appeared next, with a bright brass ring in it, and then his big wide mouth, with long white walrus tusks at either end, and then his carefully combed whiskers, and his glittering jade-green earrings, then his tall turreted turquoise turban, and at last the rest of the green smoke cleared away, and he slowly came to rest on the floor.

'I am the slave of the lamp! Ask what thou wilt, and it shall be done!' he boomed in a voice like a hollow gong falling down a deep, dark well. 'And this is a fine time to ask it,' he added plaintively. 'I was in my bath!'

'Oh, dear! How inconvenient! But bath or no bath; it's delightful to see you again, my dear Abdul!' said the Emperor Aladdin ingratiatingly.

'Likewise,' said the djinn, unbending only slightly. 'What is your wish, Master?'

'I'm in urgent need of your advice,' said the Emperor Aladdin. 'Won't you sit down?'

Abdul shook his head.

'Don't you remember? I burn through chairs,' he said. 'Advice of what nature?'

'The problem concerns my son and heir,' said the Emperor Aladdin, pointing to the cot.

'Oho, so you're a father now?' said Abdul, studying the son and heir approvingly. 'My congratulations on a fine, normal, healthy boy! How can *he* present a problem?'

'I talk,' said the son and heir pleasantly.

Abdul jerked his head up quickly.

'Who said that?' he asked suspiciously.

'Not I!' said the Emperor Aladdin wistfully. 'I wish it had been!'

'Then it was *you*!' said Abdul accusingly, turning to the Widow Twankey, a woman he had never liked; but it was apparent to him at once that he had wronged her, for she still had her fingers in her ears and her eyes tight shut.

'Odd!' said the djinn, and fixed a large green eye on the son and heir. 'Don't tell me it was *you*?' he asked flippantly, purely as a joke.

'No, no; of *course* it wasn't!'

'But it *was*,' said the son and heir cordially.

Abdul's eyebrows disappeared into his turban.

'He speaks quite fluently,' the Emperor Aladdin said apologetically. 'I was just going to tell you. That's why I rubbed the lamp. To ask you what to do!'

'The Widow Twankey is convinced it's a spell,' the

son and heir put in helpfully, 'but we think not.'

'It's certainly not an ordinary common-or-garden spell,' the djinn agreed slowly, having regained his usual aplomb. 'I don't remember having come across a case like this before . . . I have a son myself, in a quiet sort of way, but all *he* says is *boomalakka wee*.'

'Just *boomalakka wee*?' asked the Emperor Aladdin rather wistfully.

'Just *boomalakka wee*.'

'Not another word?'

'Not another word.'

The Emperor Aladdin sighed.

'You must be very proud of having a son who can only say *boomalakka wee*,' he said in a slightly envious voice.

The djinn, though slow-thinking, realized he had not been tactful.

'Well, yes; but then again, it *can* get monotonous,' he confessed. 'Though I'm not sure I'd want it any different; at least not until he's teethed. But about *your* boy, now. I'm just trying to remember something,' he added, screwing up one eye and tugging at a whisker to help him concentrate. 'It's on the fork of my tongue! I must walk up and down!'

He walked up and down, burning four holes in a valuable carpet that lay in his path.

'*Ginger!*' he exclaimed suddenly, halting in front of Aladdin imposingly. 'Does that convey anything?'

'*Whiskers?*' suggested the Emperor Aladdin, hopefully.

'No,' said the djinn.

'*Cats?*'

'Warm.'

'*An edible seasoning?*'

'Warmer.'

'My mind is now a blank.'

'I have it!' cried the djinn, slapping his forehead so hard that green sparks flew in the air. 'The Land of Green Ginger! It all comes back to me now! The Land of Green Ginger,' proceeded the djinn impressively, 'was built by a magician who was very fond of flowers and vegetables. The idea was, that when he went travelling, he could take the Land of Green Ginger with him like a portable back-garden; only fancier, if you follow me? The point is – something went wrong with the final spell. You know how it is? There's always that element of risk, even with the best incantations. Well, this final spell went wrong, and turned him into a button-nosed tortoise; and the poor man wasn't able to turn himself back!'

'Imagine that!' cried the son and heir and the Emperor Aladdin together, greatly enlightened.

'Proceed!' begged the Emperor, all ears.

'The rest of the spells worked perfectly,' Abdul proceeded, 'and while the magician was busy trying to turn himself back into a magician – which was, naturally, his immediate concern – the Land of Green Ginger suddenly rose in the air without so much as a by-your-leave, and floated off, on its own, away into nowhere!'

'Why didn't the magician make it fly back down again?' the son and heir inquired rather sensibly.

'If *you* were a button-nosed tortoise, would *you* be able to control a complicated thing like a flying-back-garden?' asked the djinn. 'Indeed you would *not*! And as nobody else knows how to control it, it just floats wherever its fancy takes it, and lands wherever its fancy takes it, and floats away again whenever its fancy takes it. It's always where you'd *least* expect it to be. For example, a tired traveller might go to sleep on a wide flat desert, and wake up with his feet under a tree, and his head on a mushroom. That would give *anyone* cause for confusion, would it not?'

'It would indeed!' the Emperor Aladdin agreed. 'But how does all this concern my son and heir?'

'What were the first words he uttered?' returned the djinn. 'Don't tell me – I *know*! He said "button-nosed tortoise"! Am I right? I see by your face I'm right! Your son,' said the djinn impressively, 'is the one chosen to break the spell of the Land of Green Ginger, and restore the magician to his normal shape! It's all been foretold, you see – nothing has been left to chance. I can even tell you your son's name. It's Abu Ali!'

'Abu Ali?' repeated the son and heir experimentally. 'I *like* it!'

'I do too,' said the Emperor Aladdin.

'And how do I break the spell, and when?' asked

Abu Ali, quite willing to set about it there and then.

'When you come of age,' said Abdul.

At this point, the Widow Twankey's voice broke in on them.

'Aladdin!' she said. 'Has the obnoxious creature gone yet?' She still kept her fingers in her ears and her eyes tight shut.

'Long ago, mamma,' said the Emperor Aladdin, diplomatically. 'The only person with us now is dear old Abdul.'

Abdul fixed his glittering gaze on the Widow Twankey.

'You know, your mother always was a little *too* active,' he said thoughtfully. 'Wouldn't she be more valuable to collectors if she were to stay like that?'

'Now, now, Abdul! I know that sometimes she makes her presence felt; but, please do nothing foolhardy,' begged the Emperor Aladdin nervously. 'She really thinks most highly of *you*!'

'Yes! So I gathered,' said Abdul drily. 'However, my time is up, Master. I must leave now. Calm your fears. All is as it should be. Peace be with you! Going *down*!'

He stamped his foot. Instantly there was another rumble of thunder, the floor obligingly split open, and Abdul sank down into it.

Less than a moment later, there was nothing to show that he had ever been there, save for a faint swirl of green smoke which hovered in the air for a moment, and then wafted out of the window.

'Well, *now* we know the answer to the problem, and we can all relax!' said little Abu Ali with satisfaction, sitting back in his cot. 'I suppose you ought to tell the Queen Mother she can take her fingers out of her ears, papa!'

The Emperor Aladdin turned to the Widow Twankey.

'Abdul's gone, mamma!' he said cheerfully. 'You can look now!'

But the Widow Twankey continued to keep her eyes tight shut and her fingers in her ears.

'Mamma!' said the Emperor Aladdin in a louder voice, tapping her with his fan. 'He's gone!'

They waited. But the Widow Twankey never so much as twitched.

'Give her a push, papa,' Abu Ali suggested helpfully. 'Just a *small* one, to begin with.'

The Emperor Aladdin gave the Widow Twankey a *small* push, and all she did was to rock gently on her feet, and then come to rest again in exactly the same position.

Little Abu Ali's face broke into a grateful smile.

'*Kind* old Abdul!' he said happily. 'He's arranged it so she *will* stay like that!'

Yes, indeed, Gentle Reader, Abdul had done exactly that!

What more impressive way to end a chapter?

Chapter the Second

*Which Explains How Abu Ali Began the Search for
the Land of Green Ginger, and Introduces the Wicked
Prince Tintac Ping Poo*

When Prince Abu Ali came of age, there was even
greater rejoicing in the ancient city of Peking,
and this time the fireworks in the palace park went
off without a smidgin of a hitch – an *excellent* omen!
– and the Grand Vizier, who was now well advanced
in age and had to wear quartz spectacles, called a
special meeting of state in the White Lacquer Room
of the Palace.

The White Lacquer Room was now enhanced by
a handsome decorative ornament, which stood on a
marble pedestal at the far end. Yes, Gentle Reader,
you have guessed correctly. It was the Widow
Twankey, and she *still* had her fingers in her ears
and her eyes tight shut; and she was dusted daily, in

the morning; for no matter how hard the Emperor Aladdin had rubbed the lamp, Abdul had never once appeared again.

It is only fair to add, however, that as the Widow Twankey was *much* more endearing as a decorative ornament than she had ever been as a Queen Mother, nobody could find it in their hearts to be as miffed with Abdul as they might have been.

The special meeting arrived promptly; as was their wont; and seated themselves in a circle on the white silk mats, with one notable exception. The Master of the Horse had been requested not to invite his friend.

Upon the arrival of the Emperor Aladdin, and the Empress Bedr-el-Budur, and the Prince Abu Ali, everyone present stood up and bowed while they seated themselves in a row on three white chairs.

Now, even though he is the hero of this tale, Prince Abu Ali had his faults, Gentle Reader; and it is my painful duty to enumerate them.

He was extremely good-looking. He always saw the cheerful side of everything.

He was too amiable; too good-natured; too kindly; too honest, and too fair-minded.

He was too considerate of other people's feelings.

He laughed too easily, and he was much too sympathetic.

He was deeply fond of both his parents.

He was never lazy, impudent, or ill-mannered.

He had never raised his voice in foolish rage, or told tales against his friends.

He was, in fact, *quite* hopeless. Nobody in the Court could foresee a brilliant future for him. They were sure he'd make a highly unsuccessful emperor.

They doubted whether he would even be able to make a good marriage; because any *real* princess was bound to find him dull and boring, and, therefore, far beneath her.

The problem presented by these serious flaws was uppermost in the minds of the special meeting when the Grand Vizier beat on the dragon gong with the ivory wand.

Everyone present looked at him expectantly, and nodded encouragingly, and gave every indication of their willingness to listen attentively to whatever he was going to say.

'Your Imperial Majesties!' began the Grand Vizier, imposingly. 'Also, Your Imperial Highness! Also, Lords and Ladies of the Court! We are met here (all except the friend of the Master of the Horse, who has been sent to his room till tea-time) to give formal voice to our humble and unworthy joy at the very important event of the coming of age of the heir apparent, Prince Abu Ali!'

Here he bowed low to Prince Abu Ali, and everyone present applauded.

Prince Abu Ali rose and graciously returned the bow. It was a charming ceremony, marred slightly by the Grand Vizier's inability to straighten up out of *his* bow.

When he had been tactfully restored to his normal height by the Master of the Horse (who never bore malice), he tapped the dragon gong again, and everyone present stopped applauding.

'We are gathered here,' he proceeded, 'to offer our ridiculously ineffectual assistance in deciding what lady, princess, or other female of suitably affluent status, shall be given the honour of Prince Abu Ali's hand in marriage!'

'Speak up!' said the Lord Chamberlain testily. 'Can't hear! What's he say?'

'You have *each* been given,' said the Grand Vizier, pretending not to have heard the Lord Chamberlain, 'a piece of paper –'

'*I* haven't!' said the Lord Chamberlain at once. 'Nor a pencil! I suppose you thought I wouldn't notice? Well, I *did*! I'm not as deaf as *you* are, Grand Vizier, and I don't need spectacles!'

This threw the Grand Vizier into such a fluster that he dropped his notes all over the floor.

While the Master of the Horse was selflessly retrieving them, Prince Abu Ali took advantage of the pause to rise and address everyone present personally.

'Forgive me, one and all,' he said courteously but firmly. 'But before we proceed further, I wish to make my position clear to avoid confusion later.'

'*Thank* you!' said the Grand Vizier, mistaking this for a vote of confidence. '*Very* handsome of your Imperial Highness! The Lord Chamberlain vents a *purely* private grievance!'

'It concerns the choosing of my bride elect,' proceeded Prince Abu Ali. 'While I am more than happy to consider all suggestions, the actual choice of my bride elect must, of course, be entirely my own.'

'No pencil!' sang the Lord Chamberlain.

'But that's unconstitutional!' cried the Grand Vizier, deeply shocked. 'It has never been permitted in the whole history of China!'

'Then it will have to be permitted for the first time,

in my case,' said Abu Ali, pleasantly, 'or there'll be no bride elect!'

'He's a dear, headstrong boy!' trilled the Empress Bedr-el-Budur dotingly, 'and his father and I *entirely* approve of his decision! Don't we, Aladdin?'

'Yes, dear,' said the Emperor Aladdin peaceably.

'Are we agreed, then?' asked Abu Ali.

'*No!*' said the Grand Vizier.

'*Yes!*' called the Lord Chamberlain, and everyone present applauded.

'Thank you!' said Abu Ali gratefully.

Thinking himself unobserved, the Grand Vizier hit the Lord Chamberlain with his fan, and the Lord Chamberlain hit him right back, knocking off his quartz glasses.

It was a most regrettable incident, only saved from further deterioration by the Master of the Horse, who discreetly confiscated both fans.

'I proceed, now, to the problem of the Land of Green Ginger,' said Abu Ali, decorum having been restored. 'As the special meeting knows, on the day of my birth, Abdul informed us that I was the person chosen to break the spell; and then departed without explaining how I am to go about it. Well, no pains have been spared to re-establish communication with Abdul, but *no* amount of rubbing the lamp has had the slightest effect. I suggest that the reason for this is that Abdul thinks we only want him to restore the Queen Mother to her former state; and we can all understand his disinclination to improve on his own handiwork.'

Everybody present nodded wisely, and then quickly shook their heads.

'It is heretofore and thus-wise my considered opinion,' continued Abu Ali, 'that if the meeting agrees never to mention the subject of the Queen Mother, Abdul might decide to appear if we rub the lamp. Which I have with me,' he added, holding up the lamp, 'because I was so gratefully confident of your wholehearted cooperation.'

This gratified everybody present so profoundly that they all nodded; except the Grand Vizier, who had sunk into an *appalling* sulk, and the Master of the Horse, who looked grave.

'May I ask the Master of the Horse why he is looking so grave?' Abu Ali inquired, sensibly ignoring the *appalling* sulk of the Grand Vizier.

'I am only too willing and anxious to tender you my unqualified support, your Imperial Highness,' the Master of the Horse assured him apologetically. 'And I believe I may say that no one is usually more open-minded and progressive than myself. But in this particular case, I can't help feeling we should let sleeping Djinns lie. Let us ask ourselves; how many *more* decorative ornaments like the Queen Mother do we need and can we afford?'

'Speak up!' piped the Lord Chamberlain. 'Can't hear! Do not encourage more fripperty-pish from the Grand Vizier! May I object now?'

'In a minute,' Abu Ali promised him, and turned to the Emperor Aladdin.

'Have I your approval, father?' he asked. 'May I summon Abdul?'

The Emperor Aladdin, though a kind and indulgent father, hesitated.

'Yes, dear. Of course he may!' prompted the

Empress Bedr-el-Budur dotingly.

'Yes, you may!' said the Emperor Aladdin peaceably.

'Thank you!' said Abu Ali.

At once everybody present put their fingers in their ears and shut their eyes; and then, remembering the Widow Twankey, hastily removed their fingers and opened their eyes again, and bravely awaited the worst.

'Abdul; if you answer this summons, we promise not to mention the little matter of the Widow Twankey!' promised Abu Ali sincerely, and rubbed his sleeve across the lamp.

There was an expectant hush that grew longer and longer; and just as everybody present was beginning to feel happier about the whole thing, a sudden rumble of thunder shook the Palace, and the floor cracked open, and the cloud of green smoke rose impressively and hovered in the air.

'I am the slave of the lamp! Ask what thou wilt and it shall be done!' boomed Abdul's voice, as he slowly materialized out of the smoke and came to rest on the floor.

'*Oooh-ahh!*' shrilled the Lord Chamberlain, realizing for the first time what was afoot; and, very sensibly for a man of his advanced years, fainted away.

'How do you do, Abdul. I notice you answer promptly enough when my son rubs the lamp!' remarked the Emperor Aladdin in modulated reproach.

The djinn looked at the Queen Mother, and put his hands behind his back.

'Well, if the lamp's rubbed when I happen to

be out, my wife is supposed to take a message,' he explained rather lamely, 'but she often forgets to tell me afterwards. Besides,' he added with more spirit, 'I don't *have* to answer the lamp! I only do it as a favour!'

'Exactly!' agreed Abu Ali tactfully. 'And I know that I'm speaking on behalf of everyone present, when I say that we're uncommonly grateful!'

'Thank you, young man!' said the genie more amiably. 'So you've come of age, at last! Well, what can I do for you, other than wish you a happy birthday? If it's about the Land of Green Ginger, I can't say more than I said before. You have to find it yourself!'

'I'm quite ready, willing, and able to do that!' Abu Ali assured him respectfully. 'But I would be grateful for one or two more clues!'

'I like your manners. You're a polite young man,' said Abdul approvingly, 'but we djinns have to use extreme caution with spells that have gone wrong! I'll tell you this much, though, you'll run afoul of the wicked Prince Tintac Ping Foo of Persia, and the wicked Prince Rubdub Ben Thud of Arabia. Never trust either of them farther than you could roll a peck of peppercorns up the prow of a perpendicular precipice!'

'I promise!' vowed Abu Ali.

'And,' Abdul continued, '*if* you do get into serious trouble with spells that have gone wrong – one invariably does – I'll allow you one rub of the lamp. Only one, mind! And before you rub it, be *sure* you really need me! Don't waste it on something trivial, like wanting a drink of water because you feel hot . . . you wouldn't believe it, but I've known many an idiot do that before now! They only do it once, though! They get the drink of water all right, but it drops out of a clear sky on to their heads, and it's in a jug!'

'I'll remember that!' Abu Ali assured him.

'Oh, and while I think of it,' added Abdul, a little *too* casually, 'not that you need be guided by everything I say – but *if* by chance you just so *happen* to call in at Samarkand while passing, you might do worse than inquire as to the whereabouts of Silver Bud, the only daughter of Sulkpot Ben Nagnag, the jeweller.'

'Why? Is she my destined bride-to-be?' asked Abu Ali alertly.

'I don't say yes, and I don't say no,' said Abdul impartially. 'I only say that *if* by chance you *do* inquire as to her whereabouts, who knows what may happen? By the way,' he added insincerely, 'I've forgotten the spell that restores decorative ornaments to humdrum and uneventful life. Does anybody mind?'

'Not in the slightest!' Abu Ali assured him promptly.

'Well, yes,' began the Emperor Aladdin uncertainly.

'Not in the *slightest!*' said the Empress Bedr-el-Budur firmly, smiling dotingly at Abu Ali.

'I'll say farewell, then!' said Abdul. 'Going down!' He stamped his foot; the floor split open; down he sank, feet first; turban last; and the usual wisp of green smoke drifted out of the window.

Everybody present drew a deep breath of relief and began feeling themselves tenderly all over to make sure they hadn't been turned into additional decorative ornaments.

'Well! The die is cast!' Abu Ali announced with satisfaction, as the floor closed over the crack. 'I will bid you a loving farewell, honoured and beloved parents, and depart on my white charger for Samarkand!'

Now by a curious coincidence, Gentle Reader, it so happened that at the identical hour that Abu Ali set out from Peking in China to seek the Land of Green Ginger, the Shah of Persia sent a politely worded message to his son, the vapid, villainous, vindictive, vengeful, vexatious, wilfully wicked Prince Tintac Ping Foo, requesting the honour of his illustrious presence on a matter of profound importance; and after the wicked Prince Tintac Ping

42

Foo had deliberately kept the Shah of Persia waiting for an hour and twenty-five minutes, he haughtily presented himself.

'Ah, Tintac Ping Foo,' said the Shah of Persia ingratiatingly, 'I want to have a friendly, man-to-man, equal-to-equal, father-to-son talk with you, my boy.'

'Oh, you do, do you?' said the wicked Prince Tintac Ping Foo ungraciously. 'Well, if it's about cheating at chess, I wouldn't bother, because I *adore* cheating at chess; I shall continue to cheat at chess; and if you *dare* try to stop me, I shall put glue in your beard!'

'Now, now, now,' said the Shah of Persia soothingly. 'It's not about chess. Cheat as much as you want to. And forget about that glue, there's a good lad,' he added uneasily. 'A joke at the expense of your elders is a joke, and I can enjoy it with the next man; but glue in a beard is glue in a beard!'

'What, then, is the purpose of this tedious confabulation?' demanded the wicked Prince Tintac Ping Foo, making no promises about the glue.

'My son,' began the Shah. 'It's time you wed –'

'Say that again and I'll stamp on your great big

gouty foot!' his foppish offspring threatened him, his nostrils pinched and pink. 'Why, in all the world, there's *no one* good enough for *me!*'

'Agreed, agreed!' the Shah of Persia pacified him. 'But you must condescend enough to take the best there is, my son, or our illustrious line will expire, will it not? Have you ever heard of Silver Bud of Samarkand?'

'No, and I don't want to!' snapped Tintac.

'Even though she is beautiful beyond all dreams?' asked the Shah temptingly. 'And her father Sulkpot

Ben Nagnag is the richest wholesale jeweller in all Araby?'

'How rich is that?' asked the wicked Prince Tintac Ping Foo in a more interested voice. 'Let me have the exact figures, and I *might* think about it – though I promise nothing, mind you!' he added quickly.

'The exact figures can be obtained from the Court Treasurer,' said the Shah of Persia. 'I would gladly leave you to browse through them at your leisure, except that my spies (who are everywhere) have secretly informed me that a rival suitor for the lady's hand has come upon the scene!'

'Who *is* he?' demanded the wicked Prince Tintac Ping Foo, scowling in a truly horrid manner.

'Prince Rubdub Ben Thud of Arabia.'

'*What?* Rubdub Ben Thud?' cried the wicked Prince Tintac Ping Foo in shrillest ire. 'That bilious butterball? Do you *dare* to tell me he has had the barefaced cheek, the nebulous nerve, the silly sauce, the conceited crust, the puny impudence, the brazen effrontery, the unabashed audacity, to pit himself against a paragon of lovably manly virtues like me?'

'I'm afraid so. Yes,' said the Shah of Persia gravely.

'Oh, har! Oh, har! Oh, har!' the wicked Prince scoffed scornfully. 'I'd like to be there when they throw him out; but it's *far* too far beneath my noble dignity!'

'I *quite* agree,' his Father said, 'and I'd laugh as loudly as you, my son; except that my spies inform me that Sulkpot Ben Nagnag looks with favour on his suit, and has invited him to lunch.'

The wicked Prince Tintac Ping Foo went as purple with jealousy as a purple stick of jealous rhubarb, and shook his fists towards the sky.

'Then woe betide Rubdub Ben Thud!' he vowed vindictively. 'He'll rue the day he crossed my path! Ho, there, slaves! My camels! My retinue! My magic sword! My jellybeans! I leave at once for Samarkand!'

And what is more, Gentle Reader, he meant it, and he *did*.

Chapter the Third

Which Explains How Abu Ali Met the Wicked Princes Tintac Ping Foo and Rubdub Ben Thud for the First Time

*T*he small, fat, footling, fatuous, infantile, infuriating, wantonly wicked Prince Rubdub Ben Thud lay back in a reinforced heliotrope hammock, singing to himself. The hammock hung between the two strongest palm trees in the last oasis but one before Samarkand, and the wicked Prince Rubdub Ben Thud's retine had camped there for the night.

He was singing a song he had composed entirely without professional assistance. It went:

> *Kadoo, kadunk, kadee,*
> *Kadee, kadunk, kadoo,*
> *Kadunk,*
> *Kadoole – oodle – dunk!*

He was accompanied on the tom-tom by his diabolically devoted devotee, Small Slave, who sat near enough to the hammock to enable him to swing it gently with one toe, thus keeping his portly master soothed, refreshed, and inspired.

'What is your *absolutely* frank and honest opinion of that last verse?' asked the wicked Prince Rubdub Ben Thud, suddenly breaking off in mid-trill, and eyeing Small Slave searchingly.

'It was as the coo of nightingales, only more

exquisite, O Prince of Song,' said Small Slave frankly and honestly. 'Pray continue these celestial tintinnabulations from your melodious diaphragm, or I shall expire before your very eyes.'

'You were a little late with the tom-tom on that last kadunk,' his master warned him, pleased but just a touch severe. 'See that it doesn't happen the next time we come to it. It should go:

> '*Kadoo, kadunk, kadee*
> – and then "Boom-boom!" from you –
> *Kadee, kadunk, kadoo*
> – and another "Boom-boom!" –
> *Kadunk*
> – "Boom-boom!"
> *Kadunk*
> – "Boom-boom!"
> *Kadoole-oodle-dunk* –
> – "BOOM!"

Do you see what I mean?'

'Only my fatuous stupidity prevented me from

anticipating it, O Prince of the Golden Voice heard only in ecstatic dreams!' Small Slave assured him humbly.

'Then we'll try it again – and this time be *extremely* careful, because I may surprise you at the end. Instead of "*Kadoole-oodle-dunk*", I'm thinking of singing: "*Kadoodle-oodle-skippety-wee*", to keep the *tonic-sol-fa* from getting in a rut. Ready? *Kadoo, kadunk, ka*wait a moment!' said the wicked Prince Rubdub Ben Thud sharply, sitting up in his hammock. 'I can hear camel bells! Can you?'

Small Slave listened carefully.

'Yes,' he said. 'Distinctly.'

'Coming here!' added the wicked Prince Rubdub Ben Thud, greatly annoyed. 'Really; there's no privacy *anywhere*! This is *my* oasis! I got here first! Go and tell them to be off!'

'Instantly, O Prince of Song,' said Small Slave, putting down the tom-tom and carefully unhitching his toe from the hammock ropes; but by this time the alien caravan was upon them, and seated on the front camel was none other than the wicked Prince Tintac

Ping Foo himself in pompous person.

The sight was so unwelcome that the wicked Prince Rubdub Ben Thud rolled out of the hammock on to his feet without even realizing he had done it.

'Ping Foo!' he hissed beneath his breath; grinding many of his teeth in rage. 'Can it be possible that he has set himself up as my rival for the hand of Silver Bud? Zounds! But soft! He approaches! Hist! Hush! Shh! Not a word of our plans, Small Slave!'

'Not a syllable!' vowed the Small Slave.

The wicked Prince Tintac Ping Foo halted his camel, and dismounted effortlessly by falling off sideways.

When his retinue had picked him up, both Princes bowed very ceremoniously to each other.

'Allah be with you and protect you, most noble and illustrious Rubdub Ben Thud!' said Ping Foo loftily.

'Allah be with you and protect *you*, most illustrious and noble Tintac Ping Foo!' returned Rubdub cautiously.

'And your *ancestors*!' said Ping Foo.

'*And* yours,' said Rubdub.

'You're not going to Samarkand by any chance?' asked Tintac Ping Foo.

Rubdub gave an airy laugh.

'Bless me, no!' he said, off-handedly. 'As a matter of fact, I'm just coming back! *You're* not going there by any chance, are you?'

Tintac Ping Foo gave an even airier laugh.

'Whatever made you think *that?*' he inquired pleasantly. 'As a matter of fact, I'm off to Yokohama to hunt yak!'

'Indeed, indeed? How too, too utterly!' said Rubdub Ben Thud with a laugh that was not so much airy as draughty. 'You won't be staying the night here, then?'

'How amusing that you should ask me that!' remarked the wicked Prince Tintac Ping Foo sociably. 'That's *exactly* what I intend to do!'

'Ooo, I wouldn't if I were you!' Rubdub Ben Thud warned him solicitously. 'The sand here is *terribly* sandy, and the water tastes *awful*! I shouldn't be surprised if there aren't a lot of mosquitoes about, too!'

'I shouldn't either,' agreed Tintac Ping Foo with

charm. 'Probably great big fat ones that never stop buzzing!'

'Then you *surely* won't stay?' Rubdub Ben Thud urged him anxiously.

'Ah, yes. Ah, yes, I will, Rubdub Ben Thud,' returned Tintac Ping Foo benignly, 'for the simple reason that it takes a much cleverer man than you to outbamboozle *me*!'

'Sir! What are you implying?' demanded Rubdub haughtily.

'That we're *both* going to Samarkand,' said Tintac Ping Foo. 'Together. In the morning. Though *you* are wasting your time, of course!'

'I must ask you to explain that remark!' said Rubdub, stiffening.

'Willingly!' said Ping Foo. 'When Silver Bud sees you, she'll die of laughter!'

'Oh, she will, will she?' said Rubdub fiercely. 'Well, when she sees *you*, she'll die of fright!'

The wicked Prince Tintac Ping Foo ceased to be polite.

'Fatty!' he said insultingly.

'Clothes-horse! Bean-pole! Fop!' retorted Rubdub instantly.

'Pudding! Sausage! Football! Tub!' answered Tintac.

'Scarecrow! Ostrich!' answered Rubdub.

'Beetle!' sneered Ping Foo. 'Why, if anyone rolled you over on your back, you'd just have to lie there till they hoisted you up again with a block and tackle!'

'*Now* you've done it!' roared Rubdub, stamping till his turban fell over his eyes. 'Umbrage has been taken! I swear by every awful oath you'll live to eat your every word!'

Quite unimpressed, the wicked Prince Tintac Ping Foo gave a short, sharp, sarcastic laugh, snapped his fingers under the quivering nose of the wicked Prince Rubdub Ben Thud, and strutted vaingloriously to the other side of the oasis, where his retinue was already making camp.

And it was at this crucial moment, Gentle Reader, that Abu Ali came riding into the oasis on his white charger.

When he went so far as to dismount and lead his white charger to the water for a drink, the wicked

princes gazed at him with deep, dark suspicion.

Abu Ali, observing their rude resentment, bowed courteously.

'Good evening,' he said politely.

'Who might *you* be?' asked the wicked Prince Tintac Ping Foo, refusing to bow back.

'Abu Ali,' said Abu Ali. 'Who might you be?'

'I could *only* be Prince Tintac Ping Foo of Persia!' said Ping Foo haughtily.

'I am your obedient servant, sir,' said Abu Ali,

instantly remembering Abdul's warning.

'And that turnip in tantrums over there is Prince Rubdub Ben Thud of Arabia!' added Tintac Ping Foo ungraciously.

'Your obedient servant, sir,' said Abu Ali across the oasis to Rubdub.

Rubdub pulled a face at both of them, and turned away in a sulk.

'Where are you going?' pursued Ping Foo. 'Not to Samarkand, by any chance?'

'No, indeed,' said Abu Ali wisely. 'I'm looking for the Land of Green Ginger. Could either of your Lordships tell me if I'm on the right route?'

'Never heard of it!' said Ping Foo unhelpfully.

'Me neither!' said Rubdub, who was all ears, sulks or no sulks.

'Then I'll stay the night here, and press on tomorrow,' said Abu Ali politely and began to unsaddle his white charger.

Now, both the wicked princes had suspected at one and the same moment that Abu Ali could *only* be a third rival for the hand of Silver Bud, so while he was washing his hands and face in the pool, the wicked Prince Tintac Ping Foo caught the eye of the wicked Prince Rubdub Ben Thud, and they tiptoed stealthily towards each other.

'He's a rival, Rubdub!' declared the wicked Prince Tintac Ping Foo in a hostile hiss. 'We must plot and plan!'

'Very well,' agreed Rubdub, in an equally hostile hiss. 'You plot, and I'll plan, and then we'll add it up and divide it by two!'

'We must poison him!' Prince Tintac Ping Foo decided, after a long plot. 'Have you any?'

'Any what? Poison? I'm very much afraid, none,' said Rubdub regretfully. 'Suppose we boil him in oil instead?'

'What oil?' inquired Tintac Ping Foo.

'Small Slave might know of some,' said Rubdub hopefully. 'Small Slave, do you know of any oil?'

'We have a little,' said Small Slave. 'Just enough for breakfast.'

'Ah, well, we won't touch *that*,' said Rubdub hastily. 'Why not shoot him with your bow-and-arrow, Foo?'

The wicked Prince Tintac Ping Foo looked embarrassed for a moment, then whispered confidentially:

'Because I often miss!'

'Then you must creep up behind him and push him into the pool, and keep your foot on his head till the bubbles come up!' suggested Rubdub with a wicked leer.

The wicked Prince Tintac Ping Foo pondered on this.

'I *like* the idea,' he admitted, 'but there's just the possibility that he might push first, and I don't like *that* idea half so well!'

'Oh, come. You have to take the rough with the smooth,' said Rubdub.

'Discretion is the better part of valour,' answered Ping Foo.

'Thrice blest is he who gets his blow in first!' countered Rubdub.

'Fools rush in where wise men fear to tread!' said Ping Foo.

'A stitch in time saves nine!' said Rubdub.

'Least said, soonest mended!' said Ping Foo.

'If your Illustrious Highnesses will permit a humble suggestion,' Small Slave broke in respectfully, 'why not pretend to make friends with the person? Invite him to supper, and drug his wine. Then, when he has fallen into a deep sleep, we can steal his white charger and depart for Samarkand. He'll never be able to *walk* there!'

'Is that the best solution?' asked Rubdub uncertainly, after a pause.

'Indisputably,' Small Slave assured him.

'Then I'm glad I thought of it!' said Rubdub.

'I beg your pardon! *I* thought of it, so *I'll* do the inviting!' Ping Foo corrected him, and nipped all further argument in the bud by strolling casually over to Abu Ali.

'Ah, there, Abu Ali !' he said, smirking with spurious charm. 'Would you care to take supper with us? Just pot-luck, so to speak; but you'd be very welcome! Very welcome indeed!'

Abu Ali smiled back at Tintac Ping Foo with equal charm.

'How very kind of Your Highness, and Prince Rubdub Ben Thud's Highness! I'd be delighted!' he said.

'Splendid!' said the wicked Prince Tintac Ping Foo. 'We'll expect you, then!'

He hurried back to tell the wicked Prince Rubdub Ben Thud of the immediate success of his plot.

They planned the supper at once, dish by dish, and the wicked Prince Rubdub Ben Thud ordered double helpings of everything for himself, which was only to be expected.

While the supper was being prepared, Small Slave mixed a powerful potion in a pewter platter, and stirred it into a jug of the best wine. It was to be given to Abu Ali at the end of the evening, and the jug had a special mark on it to warn the princes not to drink from it too.

The supper went off very well, though Abu Ali never ate anything till the wicked princes had helped themselves from the same dish first; and all would have gone as intended, except that the wicked Prince Tintac Ping Foo felt suddenly called upon to show off, and insisted on doing two rather feeble tricks with a handkerchief.

'Well, upon my *word*!' said Rubdub, who was easily taken in by tricks, even the feeblest. 'Amazing! Do some more!'

'I would be only too happy to!' said Ping Foo conceitedly. 'But for my best trick, I need a gold coin. If you care to lend me one, I guarantee to amaze you!'

The *last* thing the wicked Prince Rubdub Ben Thud wanted to do was lend the wicked Prince Tintac Ping Foo money; even for a moment or two for his best trick; but his curiosity got the better of him, and he opened his purse and handed Tintac Ping Foo a bright new gold coin *just* as Small Slave was setting the special jug of drugged wine before them.

'The wine, Your Highness,' said Small Slave significantly; but Rubdub waved him to silence, his eye glued to his gold coin.

'Thank you!' said the wicked Prince Tintac Ping Foo, taking the gold coin and biting into it carefully to make sure it was real. 'Now watch me closely!

I wrap the handkerchief around it – *so* – and wave my fingers over it – *so* – and the gold coin has now turned into a small brown pebble!'

There was an impressive silence.

'A small brown pebble?' inquired the wicked Prince Rubdub Ben Thud at last, hoping his ears had deceived him.

'A small brown pebble,' nodded Ping Foo, holding it out for him to see.

There was no mistake. It was a small brown pebble.

Rubdub gazed at it till his eyes began to water, and then said, my, how clever it all was; and would Tintac Ping Foo kindly turn the small brown pebble back into his gold coin at *once,* please?

'Ah, that's *quite* another kettle of fish, I'm afraid!' said Tintac Ping Foo with polite regret.

'Why is it quite another kettle of fish?' asked Rubdub, panic clutching at his heart.

'It's beyond my power,' said Ping Foo; adding generously, 'but you may keep the small brown pebble.'

'I don't want the small brown pebble!' said Ben

Thud hoarsely. 'I want my gold coin!'

'But the small brown pebble *is* your gold coin,' Ping Foo explained patiently.

'You mean you can't change it back?' quavered Rubdub, while spots began to dance before his eyes. 'Not never? Not nohow?'

'I'm afraid, no.'

'You mean my gold coin will *always* be a small brown pebble?'

'I'm afraid, yes.'

'By all that peals and thunders!' cried Rubdub,

trembling. 'I've been robbed! Give me back my gold coin before I punch you in one of your tiny pink eyes, you long-nosed, nobbly-kneed nincompoop!'

'Long-nosed? Nobbly-kneed?' repeated the incensed Ping Foo. 'Nincompoop? You just wait till Silver Bud has to choose between us! *Then* you'll find out what your friends have always thought of *you*!'

'Jealousy!' screamed Rubdub, flinging caution to the winds. 'He's just trying to win the hand of Silver Bud by foul means, because he knows he can't do it by fair! Jealousy, that's what it is! Jealousy of a better man!

'What utter piffle!' shouted Tintac Ping Foo. 'You're not a man at all! You're a hippopotamus!'

'*Withdraw that!*' cried Rubdub fiercely.

'On the contrary, I repeat it!' cried Ping Foo.

'Don't you dare!' yelled Rubdub.

'Hippopotamus! Hippopotamus! There! Now challenge me to mortal combat!' invited Ping Foo recklessly. 'Go on! I dare you! Challenge me!'

'Very well, I *will*!' shouted Rubdub. 'I challenge you to mortal combat! So *there*!'

'Gentlemen, this is so rash,' Small Slave interrupted unhappily. 'I *do* advise you to –'

'You fetch my sword, and keep your advice to yourself!' ordered Rubdub furiously. 'The magic sword I killed that dragon with, remember? And hurry up! I killed a dragon with that sword!' he added impressively to Ping Foo. 'I bought it from a genuine dervish!'

'I bought mine from a genuine dervish, too, and I *also* killed a dragon with it!' boasted Ping Foo, drawing his sword and waving it in the air.

'Oh,' said Rubdub, cooling down a little. 'I wonder if it could have been the same genuine dervish?'

Ping Foo suddenly stopped waving his sword in the air and lowered it slowly.

'Which kind of genuine dervish did you buy yours from?' he asked, doubt creeping into his voice.

'A whirling one, in Timbuctoo,' said Rubdub cooling down a little more.

'The one with the small shop in the High Street?' asked Ping Foo, more doubtful than ever.

'Yes,' said Rubdub, now quite cooled down.

'Did he cut hair, and do tattooing as well?'

'Yes, he did.'

'Was his name Ghoulghoul Ben Guava?'

'Yes, it was.'

They were both very pensive.

'There can't be *two*!' said Ping Foo.

'Not on the same High Street,' agreed Rubdub.

'He told me mine was the only one like it in the world,' said Ping Foo deflatedly, after another pensive pause.

'That's what he told *me*,' said Rubdub.

At this moment, Small Slave brought him his magic sword. Rubdub took it, and held it beside Ping Foo's.

'Exactly the same!' he said emotionally at last.

'But *exactly*!' agreed Ping Foo. 'I'd like a word or two with that dervish! I paid him twenty gold pieces for this sword!'

'Twenty?' cried Rubdub. 'Slumbering lobster pots! He charged me thirty! Have you killed a dragon with it yet?' he added searchingly.

'Not yet,' Ping Foo admitted unwillingly.

'So you can't be sure,' Rubdub pursued, 'that it

does kill dragons?

'No,' confessed Ping Foo. 'What an awful thought!'

'When I see that dervish again,' vowed Rubdub Ben Thud, 'I'll boil him in oil!'

'If I may be allowed a word in edgeways,' said Small Slave practically, 'Your Highnesses have made a tactical booboo. Abu Ali did not drink the wine intended for him. He rode off to Samarkand instead, as soon as you gentlemen began to squabble.'

'HE DID WHAT?' shrilled the wicked Prince Tintac Ping Foo, slapping at a palm tree in pardonable pique.

'Look!' said Small Slave, pointing.

Far away in the distance, they saw a small speck dwindling to an ever smaller one in the moonlight. It was Abu Ali galloping to Samarkand on his white charger.

'Foiled!' shrieked Rubdub. 'Foiled, by all that peals and thunders!' and he was shaken with such rage that he fell flat on his back, and it took the combined efforts of all the men in both retinues to get him back on his feet; for the wicked Prince Rubdub Ben Thud

was taller, lying down, than he was standing up, and
he never would have been able to get up unaided, not
if he had tried all night.

Chapter the Fourth

Which Explains How Abu Ali Met a Friend

*H*aving outwitted the wily machinations of the wicked princes, Abu Ali rode all night without pause, and reached Samarkand so early the next morning that no one was awake.

He climbed off his white charger in the empty market place, and sought for someone to direct him to the house of Sulkpot Ben Nagnag; for, if Silver Bud was to be warned of the approach of the wicked princes, there was absolutely no time to lose whatsoever.

When he had searched the empty market place to no avail, he heard a very cheerful voice singing in the next street.

'Awake,'
it sang,

For Morning in the Bowl of Night,
Has Flung the Stone that Puts the Stars to Flight,
And lo –!'

Here it broke off, and when Abu Ali hurried around the corner, he saw the reason for it. The singer had tripped carelessly off the sidewalk and was now lying contentedly on his back saying: *'Fight? Flight? Kite? Might? Wight?'*

Abu Ali hurried over and helped him up, though the singer did very little to assist, being quite helpless with laughter.

'I hope you came to no harm?' asked Abu Ali solicitously.

'None whatever!' the singer assured him happily. 'But thank you for asking; and a *good*, good morning!'

'Good morning!' returned Abu Ali politely.

'*Light!*' cried the singer unexpectedly. 'Listen to this!

> 'And lo, the Hunter of the East
> Has caught the Sultan's Tuwwet
> In a Noose of Light!'

'So it has,' said Abu Ali. 'Very eloquently expressed, if I may say so!'

'You liked it?' asked the singer, amazed but obviously delighted.

'Very much indeed,' said Abu Ali. 'Your own?'

The singer nodded proudly.

'Evwy word!' he said. 'Made it up this vewwy minute, as I was coming home. Fwom a party. And shall I tell you something?'

'Pray do,' said Abu Ali.

'No one has *ever* taken my verses sewiously before! *You* have an ear for poetwy! I was able to tell it at a glance! Would you care to buy a tent?'

'Some other time, perhaps,' said Abu Ali. 'Are you trying to sell one?'

'One?' exclaimed the singer. 'One? I sell *thousands*! I *make* them! Khayyam's the name – Omar Khayyam! My shop's just down the street – anything from small tents for dwomedawies, to large tents for wedding wecitals! The poetwy's a side-line, more's the pity. You *did* say you'd bweakfast with me? Vewy nice horse, that. I had a horse once. They go for days without water, don't they? No, No – that's camels. By the way, don't take it amiss, but I've forgotten your name again?'

'Abu Ali,' said Abu Ali. 'And about that breakfast –'

'No, no! Not another sillawibble, my dear fellow! You shall have it with *me* – no, I *insist*! One moment, while I find my shop –'

He looked carefully up and down the street.

'– *twy* and find my shop,' he corrected himself. 'It seems to have been done away with!'

Abu Ali looked up and down the street too, and then saw a sign directly over their heads which read

Omar Khayyam
TENTS
NO CONNEXION
WITH ANY OTHER FIRM

'I think we're here,' he suggested.

'Are we? Well, I never! So we are!' said Omar Khayyam, pleasantly surprised. '*Vewy* smart of you, Abu Ali. That's what comes of having an ear for poetwy, instead of laughing at it, like the common herd! Now where's my key? Did I forget to take it with me? Yes, I did! How pwovoking; now we'll *never* get into the shop!' he said, opening the door. 'And mind the step,' he added, falling down it immediately. 'Funny how *evewyone* does that,' he remarked as Abu Ali helped him up again. 'At least one customer in five. But business is bad evewywhere. Now, you wait here, and I'll see what there is in the pantwy!'

73

Abu Ali waited willingly because it seemed that Omar Khayyam, though a little absent-minded, was someone who could be trusted as a friend in need, and a friend in need was something he needed even more than his breakfast.

Nor was he proved wrong, because Omar Khayyam listened with sympathetic attention to the account of the trickery of the wicked Princes Rubdub Ben Thud and Tintac Ping Foo; and only shook his head when Abu Ali explained how urgent it was for him to warn Silver Bud at the soonest possible moment.

'Alas, my fwiend,' he said sadly, 'it is clear you know vewy little abut Silver Bud's father, the wapacious wapscallion, Sulkpot Ben Nagnag!'

'I know nothing whatever about him,' admitted Abu Ali. 'Will he present obstacles?'

'A hundred thousand!' Omar Khayyam assured him impressively. 'He keeps poor Silver Bud locked away like a pwisoner!'

'What? His own daughter?' exclaimed Abu Ali, profoundly shocked. 'Why?'

'The weason is all too plain!' said Omar Khayyam

sadly. 'The old wogue is tewwified she'll fall in love with some upwight young lad of no account, like you, or sometimes even me. You'll admit she could do worse. But he intends to mawwy her to a pwince!'

'Any kind of prince?' asked Abu Ali attentively.

'Oh, *no!*' said Omar Khayyam. 'He'd have to be wich, and the diwect heir to whatever thwone he's pwince of!'

'Then I have nothing to worry about!' said Abu Ali cheerfully.

'Why not?' asked Omar Khayyam in surprise.

'I'm the direct heir to the throne of China,' said Abu Ali simply.

Omar Khayyam shook his amiable head.

'I'm sowwy, but you wouldn't fool him, not for a *moment*,' he said kindly. 'Why? Because you didn't fool *me*, and I'm *much* easier to fool than old Ben Nagnag; particularly about pwinncs!'

'But I *am* a prince!' insisted Abu Ali, slightly taken aback. 'I'm the Prince Abu Ali of China!'

'And I'm Kublai Khan except in snowstorms,' nodded Omar Khayyam soothingly. 'But I know better than to twy and convince old Sulkpot Ben Nagnag of it!'

'Then you don't believe me?' asked Abu Ali frankly. Omar Khayyam shook his amiable head again.

'I like you, and I like your horse, but I don't believe you're a pwince, and you couldn't make me,' he admitted honestly. 'Are you cwoss?'

'Not at all,' said Abu Ali peaceably. 'You've done me a great service. Now I shall know better than to try to convince anyone else of it. But whether you think I'm a prince or not, I *must* find a way to see Silver Bud, Omar Khayyam! With or without the approval of Sulkpot Ben Nagnag!'

'*That*,' said Omar Khayyam, 'has been pwoved foolhardy. Why, only last spwing, a Japanese pwince climbed over the garden wall while Silver Bud was out for her daily walk around the lily pond, and Sulkpot caught him at it, and had him boiled in oil. Slowly! A *weal* Japanese pwince that was; only not wich! I wouldn't advise it, Abu Ali, I weally wouldn't!'

'Omar Khayyam!' cried Abu Ali, every inch an incognito prince. 'If you were me, would you leave an innocent maid to the mercies of the wicked Princes Rubdub Ben Thud and Tintac Ping Foo?'

'Well, of course I wouldn't, if you put it like *that*,' admitted Omar Khayyam.

'Then aid me!' cried Abu Ali.

'I *will*!' cried Omar Khayyam. 'How?'

'We must make a plan!' said Abu Ali.

But even as he spoke, villainy was afoot.

The caravan of the wicked princes had arrived in the market place and, as they passed the tent shop, Small Slave spied the white charger tied up outside, and recognized it at once.

'Master! Look!' he cried to Rubdub Ben Thud. 'There is your rival's white charger! He must be somewhere near, O Prince of Songbirds!'

'Peals of thunder! Do you see, Ping Foo? Our rival's white charger!' cried Rubdub excitedly. 'What shall we do? Kill him at once, or wait till he comes back to fetch his horse? Or both?'

'Never put all your eggs in one basket,' returned Ping Foo wisely.

'Meaning what?' asked Rubdub, bridling.

'Meaning one thing at a time,' explained Ping Foo.

'Oh,' said Rubdub. 'Then why drag in eggs?'

'I didn't,' said Ping Foo.

'You distinctly said something about eggs in a basket!' Rubdub asserted swiftly, 'and I have given strict orders that eggs are never to be mentioned in my presence!'

'It was purely a figure of speech,' said Ping Foo impatiently.

'It was meant to be personal!' said Rubdub sensitively, 'and I'll have you know that umbrage has been taken!'

'I never knew a man so touchy about eggs!' complained Ping Foo.

'Gentlemen, we digress!' interrupted Small Slave. 'That's still your rival's white charger! What do you want done about it?'

'Well, what would *you* do?' parried Rubdub cleverly.

'I'd steal it,' said Small Slave promptly, 'and leave one of our baggage donkeys in its place!'

'Give reasons for this,' requested Rubdub at once. 'In full!'

'Your rival,' explained Small Slave patiently, 'could hardly expect to be taken seriously as a suitor for Silver Bud, if he arrived there riding on a baggage donkey!'

Rubdub turned to Ping Foo delightedly.

'Isn't that *exactly* what I just said?' he demanded. 'My very words! Do it, Small Slave!'

So Small Slave changed the white charger for one of the baggage donkeys; and the caravan of the wicked princes moved on towards the house of Sulkpot Ben Nagnag the jeweller. And Abu Ali and Omar Khayyam neither heard them come, nor go.

They had, however, almost perfected an ingenious plan.

Abu Ali was to climb Sulkpot's garden wall with the help of Omar Khayyam, hide himself until Silver Bud came out for her daily walk around the lily pond, and then introduce himself and invite her to escape with him over the garden wall, where Omar Khayyam would be waiting to help them climb down again. If he was caught by Sulkpot, however, he was to whistle three times, whereupon Omar Khayyam was to run like smoke until he was far enough away not to be caught too.

'Now, are we fully agreed?' asked Abu Ali, carefully.

'Well, yes, and no,' said Omar Khayyam, still cautious. 'Suppose Silver Bud *doesn't* choose to escape over the garden wall with you? – though I'm not for a moment suggesting she might not find the idea vewy attwactive – and suppose Sulkpot *does* catch you? Where could that get you? Into a large vat of boiling oil. Take the bwoad view, Abu Ali! Are you weally sure it's *worth* it?'

'Yes, yes! A thousand times yes!' cried Abu Ali.

'Then that's that!' said Omar Khayyam, leading the way out into the street. 'Let's go!'

In the street, he stared hard at the baggage donkey for a moment, then blinked and looked again.

'Abu Ali, I don't want to alarm you,' he said, 'but your horse . . . it's shwunk!'

'Omar Khayyam!' said Abu Ali quickly. 'The wicked princes are in town! We haven't a moment to lose! Onto the donkey with you!'

'Suppose he objects?' countered Omar Khayyam uncertainly.

'No, no!' returned Abu Ali. 'He loves us! You can see it in his eyes! Now, one-two-three-HUP!'

They both jumped on to the donkey's back together, and the donkey sat down, and they both slid of backwards together.

'Well, now we know he doesn't love us as much as we thought,' said Omar Khayyam, picking himself up and dusting his trousers. 'And I nurse a pwetty low opinion of *him*, too!'

'Perhaps he misunderstood us. We'll try again!' said Abu Ali resolutely.

He caught the donkey by the tail, and lifted him back on to his feet.

'This time *you* get on first,' he said to Omar Khayyam, 'and I'll stay here to stop him if he tries to sit down again!'

'Vewy well!' said Omar Khayyam. 'But I don't like the look in either of his eyes!'

He climbed cautiously on the donkey, which immediately sat down again, this time on Abu Ali.

'Perwaps, after all, we'd get there just as soon by walking,' said Omar Khayyam, when he had helped

Abu Ali to his feet and dusted him off.

'No!' said Abu Ali, as soon as he had got his breath back. 'I refuse to be beaten! Give me a pin!'

Omar Khayyam gave him a pin.

'Now, the next time, we'll both jump on together,' he explained, 'and then hold on like fury! Is that clear?'

'It's tempting pwovidence,' said Omar Khayyam, gloomily. 'But it's clear.'

'Right!' said Abu Ali, and stood the pin on the ground, point up, just behind the donkey. 'Ready? One-two-three-HUP!'

Together they jumped on to the donkey's back and hung on like fury. The donkey, laughing quietly to himself, sat down as before; but having reckoned without the pin, he sat down on that.

Like an arrow from a bow, like a homing swallow, like a comet in the sky – like a donkey that had just sat down on a pin – he sped down the street, and Abu Ali and Omar Khayyam held on like fury.

In little less than no time flat, they reached Sulkpot Ben Nagnag's garden wall. And the curious coincidence is this. As they reached the garden wall,

the wicked Princes Tintac Ping Foo and Rubdub Ben Thud were entering the front gate with their retinues; and at the self same moment that Sulkpot Ben Nagnag hurried forth to find out how rich they were, Abu Ali scrambled up the wall by standing first on Omar Khayyam's shoulders and then on his head, and jumped down into the garden.

Chapter the Fifth

Which Explains How Abu Ali Attempted a Rescue

*E*very afternoon, just before Silver Bud went for her daily walk around the lily pond, Sulkpot Ben Nagnag's special guards, armed with large knives and long spears, marched round the garden, and, at every hundred paces – which the Captain of the Guard counted loudly under his breath – a guard was left on duty. Each guard had a whistle, and orders to blow first and ask questions afterwards.

Sulkpot Ben Nagnag had introduced this ceremony after the trouble with the Japanese prince, to nip any further sauciness of that kind in the bud.

A guard catching a suitor in the garden was entitled to two gold pieces and Thursday afternoon off, and it was only to be expected that this made them exceedingly wide-awake and alert.

Now it happened that the spot just beneath the wall where Abu Ali was scrambling up was one of the sentry-posts, and the guard on duty there was more wide-awake and alert than any of the others, for it was the first time he had ever been put on guard duty, and he was *burning* with ambition to catch a suitor.

This was not for the sake of the two gold pieces, or even the Thursday afternoon off – which he would have to spend by himself in any case – but because he longed for an excuse to blow his shiny new whistle more than he had ever longed to do anything else in the world.

His name was Kublai Snoo, and he could wiggle his ears.

Unfortunately, for Kublai Snoo, Omar Khayyam had known nothing about the guards on duty, so it never occurred to Abu Ali to look before he leapt; with the awful result that he landed fairly and squarely on top of Kublai Snoo and drove him head-first into a bed of variegated hollyhocks.

Deep down inside the holyhock bed, Kublai Snoo

first thought he had caught a suitor; then he thought an extra-large suitor must have caught *him*; but soon he began to wonder how all the peat-moss had got into his mouth, and finally assumed in a vague way that there must have been an eclipse of the sun on his Thursday afternoon off. Then he gave a half-hearted wriggle and distinctly felt his legs move, so he then assumed that he had been standing on his head to watch the eclipse when an earthquake had taken him by surprise.

Abu Ali, seeing the legs wriggle, was too kind-hearted to leave Kublai Snoo to his fate, in spite of his being a guard, so after a sharp tug or two, Kublai Snoo suddenly reappeared right-side-up in the garden with his helmet jammed tight over his eyes.

For a minute or two he was content to lie on his back and gaze quietly at the inside of his helmet, because *now* he doubted that it was his Thursday afternoon off *or* an eclipse, *or* an earthquake; and then his worst fears were confirmed. He heard a strange, sinister voice addressing him.

'If you so much as *sneeze*, you'll go back into the

flower bed!' it hissed fiercely. 'I must warn you that we are the forty thieves, and will stop at nothing! Do you understand?'

'Perfectly,' whispered Kublai Snoo faintly.

'We shall now tie you up and gag you!' added Abu Ali, sounding as ferocious as he could. 'Or would you sooner we cut you up in pieces?'

'No, I wouldn't!' said Kublai Snoo with a gulp, closing his eyes.

'Next question!' growled Abu Ali. 'Do you happen to have a piece of string *and* a handkerchief?'

'In my left trouser pocket,' whispered Kublai Snoo, very nearly in a swoon by now.

Abu Ali searched in Kublai Snoo's left trouser pocket and found both. First he tied Kublai Snoo's hands behind his back with the string.

'Now the gag!' said Abu Ali, and as he tied the handkerchief over Kublai Snoo's mouth, he added: 'Is anyone coming, Pasha Ben Hooli?' and then growled 'NO!' in a deep hoarse voice, to show Kublai Snoo what a lot of the forty thieves were attacking him.

Indeed, so occupied with his task had he become, that he failed to hear a delicate footstep approaching.

'What *are* you doing?' asked a surprised and charming voice behind him.

Abu Ali looked around, quickly, and fell absolutely and everlastingly in love at first sight with Silver Bud, who was gazing at him in wide-eyed bewilderment.

'*Oh!*' exclaimed Abu Ali, struck speechless by her beauty. And so he should have been, Gentle Reader. No one, before or since, has *ever* been so beautiful. Think of all the most beautiful blossoms you have ever seen blooming, and Silver Bud was a thousand times more beautiful than the blossom of your heart's delight.

'Why have you tied up Kublai Snoo?' she inquired politely, in a voice that was sweeter than all the songbirds you have ever heard, and all the prettiest music ever played.

Indeed, her voice so enraptured the already enraptured Abu Ali, that he had to pinch himself rapidly before he could find *his* voice.

'Because I don't want to be boiled in oil,' he answered, gazing at her in rapturous wonder.

'If you don't want to be boiled in oil,' she said very reasonably, 'what are you doing *here*?'

'I came to seek *you*!' he cried, falling on one knee. 'To serve you with my life, beloved Silver Bud!'

'Oh, dear! That's what it nearly always costs,' sighed Silver Bud regretfully. 'Who are you?'

'My name is Abu Ali,' said Abu Ali devoutly. 'And humble though I may appear to you, I have sworn a vow to rescue you from this durance vile, and take you away to happiness and freedom!'

'Indeed, though I hardly know you, I see you are

very brave,' confessed Silver Bud, touched to her tenderhearted heart, 'and, also very gallant! I couldn't bear to see you boiled in oil! Please go before they find you!'

'Never, Silver Bud, fairest of the fair!' cried Abu Ali, valiantly, rising to his feet. 'Death before dishonour! Trust me, that is all I ask! Trust me enough to fly from here with me!'

'*Now?*' asked Silver Bud. 'This very *minute?*'

'Now!' nodded Abu Ali. 'This very *minute!*'

'Certainly!' said Silver Bud, delighted. 'How?'

'All we have to do,' said Abu Ali swiftly, 'is to climb this tree on *this* side of the wall, then climb down Omar Khayyam on the other! Ready?'

'Ready!' cried Silver Bud obediently; but just as she placed her tiny foot on the first bough of the tree, an ear-splitting roar of rage shook the air, and Sulkpot Ben Nagnag came bouncing across the garden with his slippers slapping on his bunioned feet.

'Ho, there! Guards!' he was shouting wildly. 'Ho, there! Guards! Stop them! Stop them, I say! Arrest that scoundrel!'

Guards appeared like magic from every corner, and in less time than it takes to tell, Abu Ali was overpowered and dragged before Sulkpot, though he fought like a tiger and kicked the captain four times on the same leg before he was subdued.

'Caught you in the nick of time!' snarled Sulkpot savagely to Silver Bud. 'Well, what do you have to say? Explain yourself, young lady, *if* you can!'

'Well, really, father!' protested Silver Bud in a voice

of perfect calm. 'My friend and I were simply going to climb this tree to look at a bird's nest –'

'Enough! No more! Not another word!' roared her red-nosed father, and directed the bulk of his fury at Abu Ali. 'Who are you, creature?' he shouted. 'Don't answer me, you insect! I'll have you boiled alive for this!'

'You can't!' cried Silver Bud protectively. 'He's an old and trusted friend of mine! I *asked* him to go birds' nesting with me! You shan't boil him in oil! I *love* him!'

'You WHAT???' cried Abu Ali and Sulkpot Ben Nagnag together, but for very different reasons.

'I love him!' repeated Silver Bud, *quite* fearlessly.

Nobody had noticed Kublai Snoo yet.

'My ears deceive me!' rumbled Sulkpot, now quite beside himself. 'I shall choke, or something! Water! Bring me water! Ungrateful daughter! Do you realize what you said? Off to the oil vats with him! My ears and turban, I shall have a fit, a stroke, a seizure! I can feel them coming on! Away with him, guards! No! Wait a minute! Who are you, hey? What's your name, you beast, you brat, you burglar, you brute, you brigand, you blackguard?'

'Chu-Chin-Chow, laundryman!' returned Abu Ali with spirit.

'TAKE HIM AWAY!' screamed Sulkpot hoarsely, dancing with anguish on his bunions. 'Boil him in oil! Boil him in oil!'

Nothing loath, the guards obeyed.

'Stop!' cried Silver Bud, with such nobility of purpose that the guards were awed into obeying her.

Then she faced Sulkpot with her head held high.

'If you boil him in oil,' she announced clearly, 'I shall never marry anyone else, not as long as I live! I shall just pine away instead! And I mean it! I mean it! I *mean* it!'

Nobody had noticed Kublai Snoo yet; but the uproar had brought the wicked Princes Rubdub Ben Thud and Tintac Ping Foo into the garden, and they were just in time to hear what Silver Bud said.

'*What's* that?' asked Tintac Ping Foo, extremely taken aback. 'Can I believe my ears?'

'The echoes must be playing tricks!' said Rubdub

Ben Thud, taken even farther aback.

'Call some more guards!' shouted Sulkpot Ben Nagnag, having been taken even farther aback than that, and now at a loss. 'Lots more guards! I never *heard* of such a thing! Can you be defying *me*, daughter?'

'Indeed, I can!' Silver Bud assured him. 'I *am*!'

'These are all the guards we have,' said the captain apologetically. 'There *are* no more!'

'Good grief! It's that Abu Ali person!' cried Tintac Ping Foo suddenly, pointing. 'He's here before us!'

'Imposserous!' cried Rubdub. 'He has no horse!'

'What's that?' asked Sulkpot Ben Nagnag swiftly. 'You *know* this crafty cut-throat?'

'Who? Him?' shrilled Tintac Ping Foo hastily. 'I should hope *not*! Indeed! *Pff!*'

'The idea!' added Rubdub Ben Thud grandly. *'Really!'*

'In that case, gentlemen, I apologize to you for this unseemly confusion!' said Sulkpot, rapidly pulling himself together from every direction. 'Allow me to present to you my cherished daughter, Silver Bud, the bride you came to seek!'

'*Ooh!*' said Rubdub appreciatively.

'*My!*' said Ping Foo, smirking.

'Don't trust them!' Abu Ali called to Silver Bud.

'I won't!' she promised him.

'Guards, remove that knave!' shouted Sulkpot Ben Nagnag.

'Leave him alone!' countered Silver Bud at once. 'I claim the right to choose the bravest of the three to be my husband!'

'Me!' cried Tintac Ping Foo instantly.

'Me!' cried Rubdub Ben Thud, only a second later.

'Nonsense!' said Abu Ali flatly.

'Silence!' roared Sulkpot Ben Nagnag.

'The only way to prove which one is the bravest,' continued Silver Bud firmly, 'is to set all three a difficult task, and then I shall wed the one who does his task best!'

'I agree!' cried Abu Ali. 'Do you, gentlemen?'

This was met by an unaccountable silence, which the wicked Prince Tintac Ping Foo finally broke by giving a small cough.

'You said, a difficult task?' he asked Silver Bud uneasily.

'*You* heard!' said Abu Ali pointedly.

The wicked Prince Rubdub Ben Thud thrust out his low lip.

'We weren't given adequate notice of this!' he said, resentfully. 'Not so much as a hint! I refuse to commit myself until I've seen my lawyer!'

'*There* speaks a coward!' cried Silver Bud in fine scorn.

'No, I'm not!' shouted Ben Thud. 'But I have a cold! My mummie says I'm not to get my feet wet!'

'And I'm not allowed to talk to strangers!' chimed in Ping Foo. 'Otherwise, I'd take on *any* old task; and *win*!'

'Come, daughter, you are beside yourself!' fumed Sulkpot Ben Nagnag. 'Choose between these two very fine princes, for you cannot have them both!'

'Never!' cried Silver Bud. 'Not till all three have done a difficult task!'

'Extraordinary!' muttered Rubdub Ben Thud, more to himself than to those present. 'Can't think what's got into people! What next, I wonder?'

'Father!' said Silver Bud firmly. 'Set the tasks!'

'But you're not *serious*?' demanded Tintac Ping Foo in shrill amazement. 'Why, you *can't* be!'

'It just gets more and more irregular as we go along!' grumbled Rubdub. 'And I'll have you know that umbrage has been taken!'

'Ah, the trials and the tribulations of a father!' said Sulkpot self-pityingly. 'You can see that I have no choice, gentlemen,' he added apologetically. 'I'm afraid I must ask you, Prince Tintac Ping Foo, to find and bring back – bring back – a – let me see; bring back an – ah, yes – bring back a magic carpet!'

'A magic *carpet*!' echoed Ping Foo in scandalized tones. 'Whatever *for*? What on *earth* would you do with it?'

'Make it fly!' said Silver Bud, promptly.

'And me?' inquired Rubdub Ben Thud uneasily. 'What do *I* have to bring back?'

Sulkpot Ben Nagnag, never a very imaginative man, thought hard.

'Another magic carpet,' he said at last.

'Unfair! Unfair!' squealed Rubdub at once.

'And what about the upstart?' snapped Ping Foo spitefully. 'What's *he* got to bring back?'

'Yes! Make it even *more* impossible!' said Rubdub balefully.

'Don't worry – I will!' promised Sulkpot, scowling horribly at Abu Ali. 'You, creature, will bring back three tail feathers from a magic Phoenix bird, which is believed to be quite extinct by those who know!'

'Certainly!' said Abu Ali cheerfully. 'Now may I be released?'

'Yes!' said Silver Bud quickly. 'Release him, guards!'

The guards were glad to.

Still nobody had noticed Kublai Snoo.

'Magic carpet!' muttered Rubdub Ben Thud ferociously to the garden wall. 'I'd like to know where I'm expected to find an idiotic thing like *that*!'

Silver Bud laid her hand gently on Abu Ali's arm.

'I hope you'll find the tail feathers easily, and come back safely,' she said tenderly.

'I will! I promise you I will!' vowed Abu Ali with all his heart.

'Good-bye,' said Silver Bud in a small voice.

'Good-bye,' said Abu Ali, and to avoid any display of unheroic feeling, he turned away quickly and was over the wall in a jump.

Having rejoined Omar Khayyam on the other side, he wasted no time in telling him of the difficult task. Omar Khayyam, having weighed the problem gravely, said:

'Well, it's all for one and one for all; but if these magic Phoenix birds are invisible to begin with, and extinct to go on with, I'm glad it's you and not me that has to find their tail fevvers! How on earth will you start?'

Abu Ali sighed dreamily.

'How beautiful, how exquisite, how enchanting she is, Omar Khayyam!' he said. 'Her very presence scatters sunlight and happiness on the air! And brave as she is lovely!'

'Quite,' said Omar Khayyam, cordially, 'but about these tail fevvers now –?'

'My turban, yes!' cried Abu Ali. 'I've no time to lose! I must away!' And he ran to where the donkey was eating a cactus, and jumped on to its back.

'Good-bye, Omar Khayyam! I'll see you when I get back!'

The donkey swung round in a circle, and set off in the first direction that occurred to it.

'But are you sure you're going in the wight diwection?' Omar Khayyam called after him anxiously.

'No!' Abu Ali called back. 'But one's as good as another! Good-bye!'

'Good-bye!' cried Omar Khayyam, waving until Abu Ali was out of sight.

'Well, I only hope it is the wight diwection,' he added, shaking his head. 'But it doesn't *look* like it!'

But it was, Gentle Reader, it was.

Chapter *the* Sixth

Which Explains How Abu Ali Met a Green Dragon,
and How a Spell Went Wrong

When Samarkand lay far behind him, and both Abu Ali and the donkey were beginning to feel exceedingly tired and hot, they came upon a forest of tall trees, stretching away as far as the eye could see, and no doubt farther, if one but knew.

'If,' reasoned Abu Ali, bringing the donkey to a halt, and gazing at the forest, 'if I ride *round* this forest, it might take me the best years of my life! On the other hand – allowing for the fact that there are hidden dangers in forests, and perhaps dragons – if it is wide but not deep, I could ride *through* it, and be out on the other side in no time at all. I shall do this.'

Whereupon he rode straight into the forest, and soon the donkey was trotting through wooded glades where the branches knotted their knuckles together

over their heads, and small streams rippled out from
behind bushes and rippled back behind others, and
all was quiet and peaceful.

Then they came to a clearing in the forest,
and there in the clearing, dancing about and not
noticing them as yet, was a huge, horned, scaly,
scowly, nozzle-nosed, claw-hammered, gaggle-
toothed, people-hating, smoke-snorting, fire-
eating, flame-throwing, penulticarnivorous, bright
green dragon.

And, as he danced, his bright green scales banged

and clashed like cymbals, and he sang in a voice like a bright green erupting volcano:

'If you come into the woods tonight
I'll give you a horrible fright!
I'll howl and scowl
And gobble and growl!
Your hair, it'll turn to white!
For I'm a dragon,
Yes, I'm a dragon!
(That's my tail – that's what I'm draggin'!)
What'll I do?
If I meet you?
Hup-one-two!
I'll eat yer!'

Well, the donkey was so paralysed by the spectacle that it stood rooted to the spot, and Abu Ali was powerless to make it turn and run.

He simply had to sit there till the dragon did a particularly complicated hop-skip-and-turn which brought him face to face with them. At once he switched off his song in mid-sizzle, leaned his spiky elbow against a convenient tree, and surveyed them intently with his head on one side.

'You'll forgive me, I'm sure,' said the green dragon in his best party manners, 'but I don't recall having had the previous pleasure of your acquaintance! Stranger in these parts?'

'Yes,' said Abu Ali, 'and what is more, lost!'

'Lost, ha?' said the dragon, with a great show of sympathetic concern. 'Imagine that! Still, that's the way it goes! Here today, and gone tomorrow!' He smiled hard at the donkey, and the donkey dropped his ears uneasily. 'A pleasing donkey you're sitting on, good sir! Tasty, I should say off-hand! And plump!'

The donkey's ears drooped even more uneasily, and the green dragon smiled even harder back.

'I'm searching,' Abu Ali explained hastily, feeling anxious for the donkey, 'for the magic Phoenix birds, and any information you might be able to supply –'

'The magic Phoenix birds?' interrupted the green dragon expansively. 'Why, of course! I know *exactly* where you'll find them! How fortunate we met, good sir!' And here he eyed the donkey again, and was noticed by Abu Ali to lick his lips with his long green tongue. '*Most* fortunate!'

'Then would you be kind enough to direct me to them?' asked Abu Ali. 'If it's not asking too much?'

'No, no! *Indeed* it's not asking too much!' the green dragon assured him warmly. 'I'll be delighted, good sir! It's the least I can do in return!'

'In return for what?' asked Abu Ali cautiously.

'In return for eating your donkey with a lettuce salad and tomato sliced thin!' said the green dragon as blandly as a beadle.

'Never!' cried Abu Ali resolutely.

'Come, come!' said the green dragon. 'Fair's fair! *You* want the Phoenix birds! I want the donkey! Exchange is no robbery! And he'd go *beautifully* with a lettuce salad and tomato sliced thin!'

'He would not!' Abu Ali asserted. 'He's as tough as leather!'

'To you, yes,' the green dragon agreed. 'To a green dragon, no! Tasty and toothsome, tender and plump!

And this must be borne in mind, good sir; if I don't eat your donkey, I'll have to eat *you*!'

'Be that as it may,' parried Abu Ali bravely, 'and even supposing I *do* give you my donkey, how do I know you'll still tell me where to find the Phoenix birds, once you've eaten him? How do I know you *do* know where they are?'

'That's just a chance you'll have to take,' said the green dragon airily. 'Forsooth, one can never be sure of *anything* in this world, can one? That's what makes it all so exciting, I always say!'

Abu Ali pondered on his predicament for a moment, and then very reluctantly dismounted.

'Very well,' he said. 'There's the donkey. But before I leave him to his dreadful fate, tell me where to find the magic Phoenix birds!'

'Nobody knows,' said the green dragon, blithely, 'so how should I?'

'That's cheating!' cried Abu Ali hotly. 'You don't get the donkey!'

'Nonsense!' returned the green dragon stretching out a long green claw for the donkey. But Abu Ali was quicker. He slapped the donkey so hard that it gave one terrified bray and galloped off into the forest like a streak of lightning.

'*Well!*' said the green dragon, aghast. '*Imagine that!*'

'Butter-fingers!' said Abu Ali calmly. 'That's the last *either* of us'll ever see of him!'

'Yes, I know it is!' exclaimed the green dragon angrily. 'And I'm *furious,* simply *furious*! In fact,' said the green dragon, with a nasty light coming into his eye, 'I'm *nearly* too furious to eat you instead! *Nearly!*' said the green dragon, beginning to creep towards Abu Ali. 'But not *quite*! So bid farewell to this empty world of shallow pomp, because HERE I COME!'

He gave a great pounce, but Abu Ali skipped neatly behind a tree, and the dragon tripped and fell on his smouldering nose.

'Now, wait!' Abu Ali urged him. 'Pause! Consider. You're over-excited!'

'No, I'm not! I'm under-nourished!' snarled the green dragon, creeping towards him again.

He made another pounce, and Abu Ali jumped aside, and the green dragon bumped his head so hard against a knot in the tree trunk that it bent one of his horns.

'*Oooh! Ahh! Ouch!*' cried the green dragon, sitting back on his heels and rubbing his bent horn tenderly. '*Now* look what you made me do!'

Abu Ali peeped round the trunk warily.

'It serves you right!' he said. 'Do you want to bend the *other* horn? If not, stand aside and let me be on my way!'

For answer, the green dragon turned his head away indifferently and began to whistle, as if he were no longer interested in the proceedings.

Abu Ali was smart enough to remain where he was, and after a long pause, the green dragon looked back at him.

'Well, I never, did you ever!' exclaimed the green dragon in elaborate surprise. 'You're not still there? I thought you'd gone *ages* ago!'

'No, you didn't!' returned Abu Ali. 'You thought I'd be silly enough to venture out from behind this tree so you could eat me!'

'*Tcha!*' said the dragon sulkily.

'And *Tcha* to you!' returned Abu Ali.

There was another pause.

'Come out from behind that tree, and I'll show you my butterfly collection,' the green dragon invited in new, honeyed tones.

'No, thank you,' said Abu Ali. 'I have all the butterflies I need, right here in my own tum.'

'Very well then, I'll boil a kettle on my nose and we'll all have tea!' offered the dragon brightly.

'I'm not thirsty,' said Abu Ali.

'Scorpions and centipedes!' fumed the dragon in a fulminous fury, and made another sudden pounce, missing Abu Ali again, but tripping himself against a root. 'Wait till I getcha, that's all! This is a *fine* way to treat a dragon! I'll teach you to make me look undignified! Come *here*!' He made another pounce at Abu Ali, and caught his claw in a root, which tripped him up so beautifully that he sat back on his tail with an undignified thud.

'You realize that we can keep this up indefinitely, without either of us getting anywhere?' asked Abu Ali from the other side of the tree. 'I'll stop, if you will!'

'*Tcha!*' the green dragon snorted.

'And a boom-tcha-tcha! And a boom-tcha-tcha!' said Abu Ali promptly.

'Don't *do* that!' screamed the green dragon. 'I *loathe* being imitated!'

'If you mind *your* manners, I'll mind *mine*,' offered Abu Ali.

The green dragon sat down again, tenderly nursing his tail with one claw and rubbing his bent horn with the other.

'You needn't think you'll get away!' he informed Abu Ali nastily. 'Because you *won't*! The *second* you come out from behind that tree, I'll have you down in three gulps! *Two* gulps! I'm *furious*!'

Abu Ali leaned against the other side of the tree-trunk and reviewed the situation thoughtfully.

There was no doubt that the green dragon meant exactly what he said; in which case, it was just a question of time before he was eaten with a lettuce salad and a tomato sliced thin.

It was also quite out of the question to try and make a run for it, because once in the open, the green dragon would catch him easily.

Only one source of help remained to him. The one rub of the magic lamp allowed him by Abdul.

Abu Ali drew the lamp from his pocket and peeped round the tree.

The green dragon was still rubbing his foot and his bent horn, but he was watching Abu Ali intently.

'Hey there, green dragon!' called Abu Ali. 'Did you ever hear of Aladdin's magic lamp?'

'What if I did?' sneered the green dragon. 'I am an educated dragon, and not alarmed by old wives' tales and other such bucolic balderdash!'

'Do you know what this is?' asked Abu Ali, holding up the lamp.

The green dragon surveyed it disinterestedly.

'Well, goodie-goodie!' he said sarcastically. 'So you remembered to bring your own gravy!'

'This,' said Abu Ali impressively, 'is not a gravy-boat. It is the magic lamp! I have only to give it one rub, and there will be an awful rumble of thunder, the ground will split open, and a large and terrible djinn will appear in a cloud of smoke! What will you do then?'

The green dragon breathed on his claw, and rubbed it nonchalantly against his scales.

'Pardon me if I don't smile, I have a chipped lip!' he said contemptuously.

'Very well, I'll prove it!' said Abu Ali firmly. 'One! Two! –'

'*One* moment,' the green dragon interrupted rudely. 'It's only fair to tell you that I'm not being fooled by that old lamp! Instead of wasting my valuable time, why don't you act like a man and come out from behind that tree –'

'Three!' said Abu Ali, and rubbed the lamp.

For a moment the dragon looked slightly uneasy, but when nothing happened to disturb the peaceful silence of the forest, he relaxed again.

'Well? One, two, three *what*?' he jeered.

'Just you wait and see!' Abu Ali told him optimistically.

The silence remained undisturbed.

Abu Ali concealed his discomfiture behind a brave front and gave the lamp another brisk rub.

'Try blowing down it!' suggested the green

dragon disrespectfully.

The silence continued.

'Har, har!' said the dragon rudely. 'What a lamp! What do you keep in it? Glow-worms?'

Alas, Gentle Reader, Abu Ali had been so taken aback at the failure of the lamp that he forgot to keep his weather eye open. This enabled the green dragon to creep up on him unawares. Then with a roar, he suddenly pounced, and Abu Ali was just a moment too late to dodge. Before he knew it, he found himself pinned to the ground by ten large green claws.

'*Whoops!*' roared the dragon triumphantly. '*Gotcha!* How shall I start? Shall I bite you in half, or start at the toes and nibble you hither and yon?'

But the mocking words were no sooner out of his jaws when a loud burst of thunder suddenly shook the air.

The green dragon quickly turned his head and saw the ground slowly splitting open behind him.

'An earthquake!' he gasped in a horrified voice. 'Imagine *that*!'

A ball of green smoke suddenly shot up through the crack in the ground and hovered over the green dragon's head.

'Good old Abdul!' cheered Abu Ali. 'Just in time!'

'Ow, wow, *wow!*' screamed the dragon. 'A volcano too! *Mother!*'

Whereupon he turned a complete somersault from sheer cowardice and tore away into the forest as fast as his legs. could carry him, and was never heard from again, not even by postcard.

Abu Ali sat up.

'Thank you, Abdul!' he said gratefully to the green cloud in the air above him.

The green cloud was behaving in a most peculiar way, however; as if a great struggle was going on inside it.

Abu Ali waited expectantly for a moment, nothing new happened.

'Is that you, Abdul?' he inquired at last, just to make sure.

'I won't be a moment,' the cloud answered in a worried voice. 'Something – seems – to have gone –

wrong here – but – I'll – be done in a jiffy – *bother!*'

The cloud bounced about in the air, and began to bulge here and there.

'Is there anything I can do to help?' asked Abu Ali.

'Not a thing,' replied the cloud, beginning to sound a little desperate. 'Really, this is absurd – wait a minute – I've got it – no, I haven't – Nuisance, nuisance – and it always looked so easy, too!'

The cloud gave a sudden lurch sideways, turned upside down, and descended to earth with a bump, and a voice that wasn't Abdul's said: 'OOOCH!' very painfully.

Then the green smoke slowly dissolved away, leaving a very small, round, fat, knee-high, fourteen-carat, rueful, green-hued djinn seated on the grass, looking more than slightly dazed.

Abu Ali stared at him in blank surprise.

'*Who* are *you*?' he asked at last.

'Boomalakka Wee,' said the very small djinn dejectedly.

'Then what happened to Abdul?' asked Abu Ali.

'Father was busy, so I came instead,' said the very

small djinn apologetically. 'I've always wanted to answer the lamp, but he always said No, he didn't want me hobnobbing with mortals; but when you rubbed the lamp just now, he was sleeping off his lunch, so I *had* to come instead.'

He looked around him for a moment or two.

'Well, well, so this is earth,' he said, slightly disappointed. 'I was told there was more of it. You may have noticed I had a little trouble with that cloud? Answering the lamp's a lot more tricky than it looks. I forgot which was up and which was down. So the whole time I was trying to make it go down I was really making it go up. Which is why it stood still, of course. Naturally, it wouldn't go up when it knew it ought to be going down. But I think I may safely say I have mastered it, so all is well, and you can ask what thou wilt and I shall obey!'

'That's more than kind of you,' answered Abu Ali appreciatively, 'but my request has already been answered!'

'Oh?' said Boomalakka swiftly. 'By whom?'

'You!' said Abu Ali. 'I was about to be eaten by a green dragon, and you scared him away. While you were still up in the cloud, this was.'

'Oh, good!' said Boomalakka Wee, cheering up at once. 'I'm better at it than I thought! Well, now that I *am* here, can I be of any other assistance?'

'Well, if it's not too much to ask, I *do* need another donkey,' Abu Ali admitted. 'Mine ran away.'

'A donkey?' repeated Boomalakka Wee confidently. 'Nothing easier! Just watch carefully for a moment! A donkey!'

He rubbed his fingertips together and waved them in the air.

'Presto!' said Boomalakka Wee impressively. 'One donkey!'

A moment or two passed by uneventfully.

'That's funny!' said Boomalakka Wee, wrinkling his forehead. 'By rights there ought to be a donkey here by now!'

'Try again,' suggested Abu Ali. 'You know how stubborn donkeys are!'

'This one, especially!' agreed Boomalakka Wee, and rubbed his fingertips together again and waved them in the air.

'Presto! A donkey!' he repeated, rather less confidently.

This time there was a noise that sounded like *Chug*, and a little puff of dust bounced up off the ground.]

Boomalakka's chest swelled triumphantly.

'There you are, you see?' he said, his confidence restored. 'I *knew* I could do it!'

They bent over and looked.

'But isn't that a mouse?' asked Abu Ali.

'It *can't* be!' said Boomalakka Wee.

'I rather think it is,' said Abu Ali.

Boomalakka Wee examined it intently.

'Yes,' he admitted at last, in a crestfallen voice. 'It *is* a mouse! But it's not what I ordered! I *ordered* a donkey! You *heard* me!'

'I did indeed,' said Abu Ali.

'"Presto! A donkey!" I said.'

'Your exact words.'

'Exactly! My exact words! And now this mouse!'

'Never mind. Try again,' said Abu Ali encouragingly.

'Well, I would,' confessed Boomalakka Wee, 'but the thing is, if we *were* going to get a donkey, we'd have got one the first time, or not at all!'

'Am I to gather from all this beating about the bush that you won't be needing me?' inquired the mouse with icy politeness.

'You are. We won't,' affirmed Boomalakka Wee.

'Then, if it's not asking too much, would you be kind enough to repatriate me?' requested the mouse, still icily polite.

'Certainly,' said Boomalakka Wee, 'and I'm sorry we bothered you.'

He rubbed his fingertips together and waved them

in the air.

'Presto! No more mouse!' he said.

They waited for a moment.

'I'm still here,' said the mouse with a touch of asperity.

Boomalakka Wee turned to Abu Ali.

'Tell me, Master,' he said earnestly. 'Does it *have* to be a donkey? I mean, if it came to a pinch, could you make do with a mouse instead?'

'I'm afraid not,' said Abu Ali regretfully.

'So I should hope!' the mouse said tartly. 'Make-do indeed! Glory ducketts, it's not as if I *wanted* to come, in the first place! Some people, and I mention no names, might save a lot of mice a great deal of needless inconvenience if they took the trouble to get their spells right!

'The spell *was* right!' answered Boomalakka Wee hotly. 'Except that I ordered a donkey.'

'I am no doubt rather dense,' said the mouse with mounting truculence. 'May we take it a step at a time? The spell was right, except that you ordered a donkey. And what did you get? You got a mouse.

So *somebody* blundered. It can't possibly be you. So, I suppose it's *me*, for not being a donkey?'

'I didn't say that!' returned Boomalakka Wee swiftly. 'But what I *do* say now, is that I've known mice who kept their place, and I've known mice who didn't; and the mice I admire least are the mice who think they're ever so bright and witty!'

'To which type of mouse do you infer that I belong?' demanded the mouse icily.

'If the cap fits, wear it!' said Boomalakka Wee.

'Gentlemen, gentlemen,' Abu Ali restrained them peaceably.

'Gentlemen?' snapped the mouse, rounding on Abu Ali. 'I'd have thought *you'd* have known better! Can't you tell a lady when you see one?'

'I beg your pardon, ma'am,' said Abu Ali hastily.

'Granted as soon as asked,' the Mouse replied in a slightly mollified voice. 'And now may I go home? I have friends who will become anxious!'

'Certainly!' Abu Ali assured her gallantly. 'Send the lady home, Boomalakka Wee!'

'I will when I can get a word in edgeways,' said

Boomalakka Wee sulkily, and made the magic pass again.

Nothing happened that hadn't happened before – which was nothing – and Boomalakka Wee blushed bright green with annoyance. He made the magic pass three times more, and then he sat down and cupped his chin in his hands.

'I can't think *why* it doesn't work!' he said disconsolately. 'I've watched father often enough!'

The mouse gave a rather hollow laugh.

'It's come to a *pretty* pass, I *must* say,' she declared, 'when a lady has to start life afresh in a strange land, without so much as a word of warning or a crumb of cheese!'

'I suggest,' said Abu Ali helpfully to Boomalakka Wee, 'that you go back home to Abdul, explain the situation, and ask *him* what to do.'

Boomalakka Wee brightened.

'Of course, yes!' he said, jumping. up. 'I should have thought of it myself!'

'How,' inquired the mouse, unexcited, 'do *you* propose to get back, when you can't even send *me* back?'

Boomalakka Wee looked daggers at her.

'You *do* pour cold water on *everything*, don't you?' he said resentfully. 'Well, just you watch, that's all!'

He stamped on the ground with one foot.

'Gowing *down*!' he cried ringingly.

Nothing happened. Nothing whatever.

'So now,' said the mouse with morbid satisfaction, '*no one* can get back. We're here for ever. What fun. Tra-la-la. But, if ever I *do* get back,' she added pugnaciously, 'someone will answer for this! I mention no names, but just watch where my eyes rest!'

'Wait,' said Abu Ali soothingly. 'I have the solution. It's very simple. I'll rub the lamp again, and Abdul will answer it, and then he'll put everything right!'

'No,' said Boomalakka Wee in a small, sad voice. 'No, he won't. He can't. Not till I get back. The lamp works for only one person at a time; and as I can't get *back*, father can't get *here*!'

'It just gets more and more gay,' said the mouse lugubriously. 'I can't remember when I've laughed so hard. Hey-nonny-no.'

'To sum up,' said Abu Ali without reproach, 'we

123

are lost in the middle of the forest. We have no way of getting out except by walking. And we may run across a green dragon any moment now. Otherwise, everything's splendid.'

'Yes, indeed, and it has even a bright side,' agreed the mouse, eyeing Boomalakka Wee expressively. 'You could well say that you lost a donkey, only to gain an even bigger one.'

Chapter the Seventh

Which Reveals the Awful Villainy of the Wicked Princes Over a Magic Carpet

Over the brutally blistering, baking, bleaching Arabian Desert rode the wicked Prince Tintac Ping Foo and his retinue, and the sun beat down, and the dust blew about, and the camels coughed, and the wicked Prince Tintac Ping Foo was in a shocking temper, for the sand had got up his nose, which is more than a man can stand.

Hot as he was, however, and angry as he was, the wicked Prince Tintac Ping Foo was still able to feel pleased with himself because, while he was still in Samarkand, he had found out through spies that, in the *exact* centre of the Arabian Desert, was a carpet shop; and in the carpet shop were magic carpets galore to be had for the modest sum of five hundred gold pieces.

He was doubly pleased with himself for having *then* arranged for *his* spies to tell the spies of the wicked Prince Rubdub Ben Thud that the shop was in the middle of the *Sahara* Desert; and he was triply pleased with himself because the last sight to meet his eyes as he left Samarkand, was the wicked Prince Rubdub Ben Thud hurriedly setting off for the Sahara Desert, which, apart from being an unbelievably long way off, had *no* carpet shop whatsoever.

The wicked Prince Tintac Ping Foo considered this intrigue one of his cleverest, and his retinue had to listen to the story well over seventy or eighty times, and as they were expected to laugh just as heartily every time they heard it, their tempers (though controlled) were soon in as shocking a state as their lord and master's.

Soon a spot appeared on the shimmering horizon of the desert. As they drew near it, it grew larger, and as it grew larger, it began turning into palm trees, and the retinue of the wicked Prince Tintac Ping Foo gave three weary cheers, for this was the oasis where the magic carpets were sold.

'*Heigh-ho!*' sang the Wicked Prince Tintac Ping Foo. '*Heigh-ho-tiddle-hi-tiddle-ho!*

> 'I'm brutal and beastly and bad!
> I behave like a pig to my mother!
> I'll knock out your tooth
> just to prove I'm uncouth!
> Keep still and I'll knock out another!
> I'm florid and horrid and mean!
> No one could ever be meaner!
> To eat a small goil
> I first boil her in oil!
> Where's my dinner?
> Has anyone seen her?'

'Bravo! Very fine! More!' cried his retinue.

And what is more, they almost meant it.

Oh, Gentle Reader, with what triumph did they ride into that oasis! And as they entered it from the *right* side, with what triumph did the retinue of the wicked Prince Rubdub Ben Thud enter it from the *left* side; so that they all met in the middle, right outside the shop that sold magic carpets.

The wicked Prince Rubdub Ben Thud leaned out of his litter with a smug smile all over his fat face, and there was plenty of room for it.

'Coo-ee ! *I* see you!' he cried to the wicked Prince Tintac Ping Foo. 'Fancy meeting *you* here!'

The wicked Prince Tintac Ping Foo went ashen white from sheer fury.

'Oh, *no*! It's not *true*!' he choked, and his teeth chattered like magpies. 'It's a mirage! An optical illusion! Astigmatism! Convergent strabismus! Snow blindness! A delusion! I can't stand it! I shall have to scream!'

'Come, come! Not in front of the servants!' Rubdub reproached him gaily. 'Nor have your eyes deceived you! It's dear little old me myself in person!'

'*How did you get here?*' demanded Ping Foo, trembling violently from head to toe.

'In a litter!' giggled Rubdub. 'My, my, Ping Foo, I was hardly able to keep a straight face when *your* spies told *my* spies that this carpet shop was in the *Sahara* Desert! And when you thought I *believed* you, a very hearty laugh was had by all! A *very* hearty laugh!'

'This means war! Defend yourself, Thud!' trumpeted Ping Foo in a tremolo obligato. 'We will fight it out, here and now, till one of us falls, never to rise again!'

'Fally-diddle-di-do!' returned Rubdub in the best of tempers. 'We'll do nothing so footle! Pull yourself together, Ping Foo. I've as much right to buy a carpet here as you have, haven't I?'

Now this was so reasonable that, if only to save face, the wicked Prince Tintac Ping Foo had to pretend he agreed.

'Well, we're *here*; so least said, soonest mended,' he

conceded with poor grace. 'Let's go and buy our silly old carpets!'

Rubdub was scientifically assisted out of his litter by his long-suffering retinue, and side by side, avoiding each other's eye, the wicked princes pranced into the carpet shop.

Not unnaturally for a carpet shop, there was a wide variety of carpets on display inside, of every sort and size and colour; but none of them looked particularly magic. Nor was there anyone behind the counter, so the wicked Prince Tintac Ping Foo rapped on it sharply with his knuckles.

'Hullo!' he cried impatiently. 'Attention!'

'Really!' said Rubdub severely. 'The service here is terrible! Bang on the counter again, Ping Foo!'

'Bang on it yourself!' answered Ping Foo tartly, having banged on it harder than he meant to, and made his eyes water.

Rubdub clapped his hands loudly together instead.

'Ho, there!' he called loudly. 'Will somebody kindly sell us a carpet before we leave in a huff?'

At these words the curtains at the back of the

shop parted, and Aladdin's wicked Uncle Abanazar hurried out.

You recall, Gentle Readers, that he had been banished to Persia for his bad behaviour in Peking? Well, the Persians had banished him too; and here he was, very much come down in the world and rather gone to seed, selling carpets in the middle of the Arabian Desert and barely able to make ends meet.

'What's that?' he cried pathetically. 'Did I hear right? You really want to buy a carpet? Pardon me, gentlemen! I thought at first you were just two more camel drivers! They never buy a thing – just mess the place up and waste my time! Make yourselves comfortable, gentlemen! Pray sit! I have an *exquisite* line here in Persian carpets, in three convenient sizes, and with every order of a thousand gold pieces, we give away *absolutely free a* special doormat with "MOTHER" on it in pink wool! It really doesn't pay us, but we want the goodwill of the customer above all else! You know our motto? You don't? "The customer is always right!" That's our motto, gentlemen! And if you don't like your carpet, why, all you have to do is bring it back and we'll change it – we'll be *glad* to change it! It's all part of the Wishwash Ben Ragbag Carpet Company's policy for bigger and better customers, because – as we say in our motto – the customer is always right, which is why we give away the doormat free –'

'*Desist!*' cried the wicked Prince Tintac Ping Foo in a sizzling frenzy. 'I came here to buy a magic carpet! One that flies! Show me what you have!'

'And show me, too!' added Rubdub Ben Thud.

'And be sure they're of a slightly better make than the ones you show *him*!'

'I want the finest you have in the shop!' Tintac Ping Foo put in quickly. 'Expense no object! Serve this portly pipsqueak second! *I* asked first!'

'You did not!' said Rubdub fiercely. 'We both asked together; but I have a more lovable personality, so of course he'll serve me first!'

'Well, gentlemen,' began Abanazar awkwardly, 'you've put me in rather an embarrassing position –'

'Stop that infernal chatter and show me a magic carpet!' ordered Tintac Ping Foo imperiously. 'I'm in a hurry!'

'The fellow was addressing *me*, Ping Foo!' said Rubdub furiously. 'So *kindly* wait your turn! What *manners*!'

'The point *is* –' said Abanazar regretfully.

'Never you mind about my manners!' said Tintac Ping Foo sharply. 'Yours aren't so perfect that you can criticize your betters! You *shan't* be served first; so sucks boo!'

He dragged Abanazar away by the arm.

'Oh, no you don't!' shouted Rubdub, seizing Abanazar by the other arm and dragging him back. 'Show *me* your magic carpets, fellow; quick and lively, do you hear?'

'But, gentlemen!' cried Abanazar tearfully. 'You won't *listen* to me! I'm trying to tell you that all I have is the *only* magic carpet left in the world! Now will you *please* let go of my arms?'

The wicked princes let both his arms go at once.

'*You've what?*' asked Tintac Ping Foo in a horrified whisper.

'*The only one left in the world?*' echoed Rubdub Ben Thud in an equally horrified whisper.

'I'm sorry, gentlemen! I really can't *tell* you how sorry I am! But the only one of its kind left in the world is a Turkish eight-by-ten in brown and white for nine-hundred-and-ninety-nine-and-a-half gold pieces!'

'*I'll take it!*' shrieked both the wicked princes together, and began scrambling madly for their purses.

'*Don't sell it to him!*' screamed Tintac Ping Foo, counting out his gold pieces so rapidly that half of them fell to the floor. '*It's mine! It's mine!*'

'*It's not! It's mine!*' screamed Rubdub Ben Thud, turning purple in the face. '*Get away, Ping Foo; you thief, you!*'

Abanazar stood gazing at them with his mouth open, wishing he had asked twice as much for the magic carpet; but after a moment or two, it began to dawn on him that Rubdub Ben Thud's purse, full of gold as it was, didn't hold nine-hundred-and-ninety-nine-and-a-half gold pieces.

Indeed, this had also begun to dawn on Ben Thud, and he began to count more slowly, and his excitement began to ebb, because now that he came to think of it, he had only brought five hundred gold pieces with him.

He glared at Tintac Ping Foo with jealous loathing, and then he saw that Tintac Ping Foo was counting more slowly too, and had an equally worried look on his face.

'How many gold pieces do you have in your purse, Foo?' asked Rubdub at last, in a quavering voice.

Tintac Ping Foo looked up and glared at Rubdub

with jealous loathing.

'Five hundred,' he admitted with poor grace. 'So you win, Thud! Go on and buy your old carpet, and I hope you roll off it when it's up very high!'

Rubdub shook his head mournfully.

'No,' he said. ' I don't win. All *I* have is five hundred gold pieces.'

'Can I interest you gentlemen in two other carpets, then?' asked Abanazar quickly. 'I have two Bokhara rugs for four-hundred-and-ninety-nine-and-a-half gold pieces each! Of course, we can't guarantee any magic for *that* price, but you still get the free doormat with "MOTHER" on it in pink wool, and you'd *laugh* if you knew what a small profit I make on the sale –'

'Will you be *quiet*?' snarled Tintac Ping Foo. 'I'm trying to *think!*'

'I've *thought*,' said Rubdub Ben Thud gloomily.

'Was there a result?' asked Tintac Ping Foo.

'No,' said Rubdub, and sat down despondently on a pile of the free doormats with "MOTHER" on them in pink wool.

'I can see what'll happen! That awful upstart will

find the three tail feathers and win Silver Bud! I wish I'd never let you talk me into it in the first place!'

Small Slave, who had been watching their every move, stepped forward.

'Pray do not despair so easily, your Highness,' he murmured respectfully. 'If this *is* the only magic carpet left in the world then Sulkpot Ben Nagnag set you both an unfair task.'

'Well, we all know *that*!' snapped Rubdub irritably.

'Yes, tell us something we *didn't* know!' snapped Ping Foo.

'Hear me out,' requested Small Slave. 'If it *hadn't* been an unfair task, you would *each* have flown back on your *own* magic carpet, would you not?'

'If beggars were horses,' said Ping Foo unnecessarily, 'wishes would ride!'

'Agreed,' said Small Slave, patiently. 'But on the other hand, if you *both* buy this carpet and fly back on it together, you'll *both* have fulfilled *your* part of the bargain, and Silver Bud will have to choose between you!'

'Peals of thunder!' exclaimed Rubdub, brightening up.

'Of course!'

He jumped off the pile of doormats and scooped his gold pieces together.

'Here's *my* five hundred!' he said quickly. 'Now put down yours, Foo! If we fly back on the carpet, we'll get there *long* before that Abu Ali upstart! Kadoo, kadunk; what a *brilliant* solution! My, *my*! How *lucky* I thought of it in time!'

And that, Gentle Reader, was how the wicked princes came to be the incompatible owners of the only magic carpet left in all the world.

Chapter the Eighth

Which Explains How Abu Ali Consulted Nosi Parka and Gained Fresh Hope

*T*he sun was beginning to set over the forest; but it was still very peaceful and pleasant, with never a sign of a green dragon or a donkey.

Through the trees, keeping close together, walked Abu Ali, Boomalakka Wee and the mouse; and they were lost.

They had been walking for quite some time now, but nobody had spoken to anyone else much; for Abu Ali was racking his brains for a way to find the Land of Green Ginger; and Boomalakka Wee was still humiliated because the spells hadn't worked; and the mouse had decided she was the put-upon victim of a contemptible conspiracy. Indeed, she was just about to sit down and refuse to budge another inch until presented with a written apology, when they suddenly came out of the trees on to a grassy bank, and there in front of them lay a huge, wide, languidly rolling river.

'That's a river, that is!' Boomalakka Wee informed them importantly. 'Some of the wet kinds are often made of water!'

'*Some* people,' said the mouse, 'mentioning no names, can tell a river when they see one, and don't need it demonstrated. I allude, however, to people of resource and reliability; not fledgelings who start spells they can't finish!'

'Abu Ali!' said Boomalakka Wee in exasperation. 'I hate to say it, but the time has come for that mouse to be shown her place, put in it, and made to stay there!'

'Hush!' said Abu Ali, lifting up his finger. 'I can hear someone singing! Can you?'

Boomalakka Wee and the mouse strained their ears, and sure enough, a voice came faintly down the wind.

'*A life on the ocean wave!*' it sang. '*A life on the ocean wave! Tantivvy, tantivvy, tantivvy; a-shrimping*

we will go!' And the next minute, a little skiff with a
red sail came round the bend of the river.

'We're saved!' cried Abu Ali joyfully. 'Wave! Attract
their attention!'

'Oh, yes – let's!' cried Boomalakka Wee excitedly.
'I want a ride in the boat! I want a ride in the boat!'

'Well-informed people say *voyage,*' said the mouse,
'and it's a *ship*, not a *boat*. But let it pass. It fell on
deaf ears.'

'Halloo, there!' cried Abu Ali, waving. 'Ship ahoy!'

'Halloo, there! Ship ahoy!' cried the mouse.

'Halloo, there! Boat ahoy!' cried Boomalakka Wee. 'I want a ride!'

'Halloo there!' a cheerful voice returned, and someone in the skiff stood up and waved back. 'Stand by, ye lubbers ! I'm coming ashore!'

The little skiff began sailing towards them, and very soon they could make out a young man at the tiller in a red-and-white striped jersey and a wide straw hat. He had a sword in his belt, a telescope under his arm, a parrot on his shoulder, a compass on his wrist, and a small copper weathervane on the end of his umbrella.

Abu Ali ran down to the edge of the river, and as soon as the skiff was near enough, the young man threw him a rope and Abu Ali pulled the skiff against the bank.

'Heave ho!' called the young man heartily. 'Who might *you* be?'

Abu Ali told him. 'And we're lost,' he added, 'all three of us! Who are you, sir?'

The young man thumped himself proudly on the jersey.

'Sinbad the Sailor, me hearties!' he announced. 'Son of *the* Sinbad! *Oh, a life on the ocean wave's the only life for me!* What can I do for you, matey?'

'We want to get to the other side of the river!' said Abu Ali. 'Will you ferry us there?'

'Glad to, matey; but why? There's only more forest,' said Sinbad, 'though not as much. And on the other side of *that* is the Arabian Desert. So they say. But if you're coming aboard ye'll have to shake a leg, ye pesky landlubbers!' he added. 'There's a squall coming up on the port bow!'

'Which *is* the port bow?' asked Abu Ali.

'Whichever you prefer,' said Sinbad generously. 'I find that either answers admirably. All aboard that's coming aboard!'

'Help me up! Help me up!' cried Boomalakka Wee excitedly.

'Not that it matters,' said the mouse to no one in particular, 'but it's usual for women and children to come first, at sea.'

Abu Ali lifted her aboard at once, and then hoisted Boomalakka Wee over the side, and then pushed the skiff off with one foot and climbed aboard himself.

'*Heave ho! Achors aweigh!*' sang Sinbad, pulling hard at the sail. 'Splice the main-sail and spank the jib-boom! Hard a-helm! Thar she blows! Pop goes the weasel! We're off on the rolling main!'

'It's still just a river to me,' said the mouse to herself, and then added swiftly to Boomalakka Wee: 'That's right! Go on! Say I'm pouring cold water on everything!'

'Mouse!' said Abu Ali sternly, his patience at an end. 'For the last time, stop this bickering! *And* you, Boomalakka Wee!'

'Ooh, I never said a *word!*' protested Boomalakka Wee.

'No, but you were *thinking* dozens of them!' said the mouse. 'All rude!'

'You see that? *She* started it!' said Boomalakka Wee.

'I did not!' said the mouse angrily. '*You* did!'

'I don't care who started it!' said Abu Ali loudly. 'All I said was, there'll be no more bickering from either of you!'

'That's the stuff, matey!' said Sinbad approvingly.

'Terrible thing, mutiny!'

Boomalakka Wee and the mouse marched to opposite ends of the skiff and sat with their backs to each other.

'Where are you bound for, shipmate?' asked Sinbad conversationally.

'The Land of Green Ginger,' said Abu Ali.

'Land of Green Ginger?' repeated Sinbad. 'Never heard of it!'

Abu Ali sighed. 'Nor has anyone else,' he said regretfully. 'It has no fixed address. It moves about.'

'That's what I'd call elusive,' said Sinbad, shaking his head. 'You'd be more successful looking for a needle in a haystack!'

He thought a minute and then suddenly brightened.

'Well, shiver my timbers for a simpering sea-cook!' he exclaimed. 'Why, we're passing the very man for you! Avast there, me hearties! Hard a-port! Tack to the starboard bow!' He tugged at the sail till the skiff veered straight for the opposite shore.

'Over there, somewhere,' directed Sinbad, waving vaguely at the trees beyond the shore, 'you'll find

Nosi Parka the egg head. He has a crystal ball, and he only has to look in it to know what's going on all over the world! If *he* can't tell you how to find the Land of Green Ginger, take it from me, matey, *Nobody* can!'

At this, fresh hope filled Abu Ali's breast, for it really seemed that at long last the Land of Green Ginger was almost within his grasp. He thanked Sinbad profusely, and impressed upon him that if ever Sinbad was in China he must be sure to call at the palace, where he would be very welcome indeed. Sinbad thanked him with equal profusion, but doubted if he'd ever get as far as China unless someone invented a way of doing it by river, as the open sea made him deathly sick.

By this time, the skiff had reached the opposite bank, and Abu Ali, having thanked Sinbad all over again, helped down Boomalakka Wee and the mouse, and when they had both said *their* good-byes, Abu Ali gave the skiff a push and watched it tack out into mid-river once more. Then they all waved to Sinbad, who waved his umbrella back until the little skiff disappeared round the next bend.

'Now to find the cave!' said Abu Ali cheerfully, and he set off into the forest, followed by Boomalakka Wee and the mouse, who were, I regret to say, still haughtily ignoring each other.

This time it was much easier to find their way among the trees, because the grass had been trodden into a well-worn path; and when they had been following it for a while, they came to a large notice nailed to a tree, and the notice asked:

WHAT DOES THE FUTURE HOLD FOR YOU?
CONSULT NOSI PARKA THE EGG HEAD!
FEE NOMINAL! RESULTS FEENOMINAL!

'Aha! We've come in the right direction!' said Abu Ali with great satisfaction. '*Now* which way do we go?'

At this, the notice on the tree flapped over on a hinge, and underneath was another notice which said:

FOURTH TREE TO YOUR RIGHT, TURN LEFT,
AND YOU CAN'T MISS IT!

'Thank you very much!' said Abu Ali gratefully.

At once, the notice flapped over, revealing another underneath which read:

THE PLEASURE IS ENTIRELY MINE!

'Puns aside, I don't know when I've seen a politer notice,' confessed the mouse. 'Unless it's worked by strings!'

'The fourth tree on our right,' said Abu Ali carefully. 'That'll be *that* one – then turn left and we can't miss it!' and off they went.

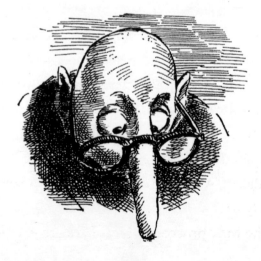

In no time at all they reached a cave, and sitting cross-legged in front of it wrapped in a kaleidoscopic kimono was Nosi Parka the egg head himself, and he had the baldest head and the largest nose in the world; but the rest you will have to imagine for yourself, Gentle Reader, as he is quite impossible to describe.

'Ah, there you are, Abu Ali,' he said in a mild and kindly voice. 'I've watched you in my crystal for quite some time now. The Land of Green Ginger's not as easy to find as you bargained for; is it? Still, never mind . . .'

Here he broke off and fixed his wise old eye severely on the mouse.

'Madam, I read minds,' he reminded her decorously. 'So I know what you're thinking. But don't you dare say it! I'm sensitive about my nose!'

The mouse had the grace to blush and look away hurriedly.

'*And* about my bald head!' Nosi Parka added to Boomalakka Wee, who blushed and looked away hurriedly too.

'By the way,' proceeded Nosi Parka to Abu Ali, 'my

terms are strictly cash. A silver piece to read your fate in my crystal, my fine gentlemen, and it's money well spent!'

'Certainly!' said Abu Ali willingly, taking out his purse. He handed Nosi Parka a silver piece, and Nosi Parka tossed it over his shoulder into the back of the cave without even biting it to see if it was good.

'Personally I have no use for money,' he explained. 'But people never value advice they haven't had to pay for! Now, listen closely, Abu Ali!'

He bent over the crystal till the tip of his long nose was touching it, and gazed into it intently.

'I see,' he said at last, very slowly and carefully. 'I see a tall thin man and a small fat man doing something very odd with a carpet. Lean forward and look, my fine gentleman. And if you listen hard, you'll even hear what they're saying!'

Abu Ali peered into the crystal; and there, as clear as daylight, were the wicked Princes Rubdub Ben Thud and Tintac Ping Foo, and they were unrolling the magic carpet outside the carpet shop in the Arabian Desert, and they were looking very pleased

150

with themselves indeed.

'It's the wicked princes!' exclaimed Abu Ali in dismay. 'And they've found their magic carpets already!'

'Don't talk!' reproved Nosi Parka. 'Just listen!'

Abu Ali listened, and heard the voice of the wicked Prince Tintac Ping Foo quite plainly.

'Don't you *dare* get on before me, Ben Thud!' he was calling excitedly. 'We both get on together! Are you ready? *One – two – three!'*

They both stepped on to the magic carpet.

'Now!' Ping Foo said gleefully. 'Now for the magic words! *Take us, carpet,'* he recited solemnly, '*to the house of Sulkpot Ben Nagnag!'*

They braced themselves expectantly, but the carpet appeared not to have heard.

'It's in Samarkand, carpet!' explained Ping Foo impatiently. 'Near the market place! We'll tell you where to, stop!'

The carpet never so much as twitched.

'That's an *order*, you silly carpet!' said Rubdub. 'Take us there at *once!*'

There was a faint flip at one corner of the carpet.

Ping Foo's face began to redden with annoyance.

'Ben Thud!' he said through his teeth. 'I believe we've been sold another pup! *Hey, shopkeeper!*'

Abanazar came out of the shop.

'What sort of magic carpet do you call this?' demanded Rubdub Ben Thud indignantly. 'I thought you said it flew?'

'It does too!' returned Abanazar stoutly. 'I had it out only this morning, and it flew *beautifully*!'

'Then why doesn't it fly *now*?' snapped Ping Foo.

'Because there's too much weight on it!' returned Abanazar. 'No carpet could carry *that* weight!' he added meaningly, looking at Rubdub Ben Thud.

'Retract that!' ordered Rubdub, colouring. 'Impertinent peasant!'

'Well, if you gentlemen will step off for a moment,' said Abanazar, 'I'll prove it!'

The wicked princes eyed each other mistrustfully, and then carefully counted One – two – three and stepped off together.

Abanazar stepped on to the carpet.

'Once round the house, please, carpet,' he said,

'and no bumps when you land.'

Right under the very noses of the wicked princes, the magic carpet rose gracefully into the air, sailed effortlessly round the carpet shop, and came lightly down to earth again.

'There!' said Abanazar, stepping off. 'What did I tell you?'

The wicked princes looked at each other without affection.

'*One* of us,' said Ping Foo clearly and pointedly, 'will have to go back to Samarkand by litter!'

Rubdub Ben Thud said nothing, but he looked *daggers*.

'Well?' asked Ping Foo. 'What are you waiting for? I'd start now if I were you!'

'Yes, I think I will. Ta-ta, Ping Foo,' said Rubdub with deceptive meekness, and pretended to turn away; and then suddenly, without warning he kicked Ping Foo on the shin, and while Ping Foo was hopping on one leg yelling: 'Ahh-ooow!' Rubdub jumped swiftly back on to the carpet.

'Take me to the house of Nagnag Ben Potsulk,

carpet!' he shouted quickly. 'No, no! I mean to the House-House of Nagsulk Ben Pot! – No, no! I mean to the Potpot of Sulkhouse Ben *Ouch*!'

For by now Ping Foo had recovered his balance and *hurled* himself head-first at Rubdub with such frenzy, that all Abu Ali could see in the crystal was a seething whirlwind of arms and legs and turbans, and the air was filled with grunts and groans and wails and screams and many unkind words.

'A shameful exhibition!' said Nosi Parka disapprovingly as the crystal clouded over. 'Now let us try for the Land of Green Ginger!'

He bent over the crystal and frowned in concentration, and soon another picture appeared in it. It was a nice little bald old lady trying on a wig, and when she found herself observed, she looked very embarrassed and dropped the wig. Then the picture changed to a flock of geese; then some camels; then there was a rather pretty stretch of bright blue sky; and then an apologetic sign appeared, saying: 'NORMAL SERVICE WILL BE RESUMED ANY MOMENT NOW I THINK', and at last the picture of bright blue sky reappeared in the crystal. At first it was just ordinary bright blue sky; but after a moment, a blob appeared in the distance, and then the blob began to grow bigger and bigger and broader and broader and greener and greener, until at last there could be no doubt in anybody's mind that it was the Land of Green Ginger moving from one place to another.

'*There* it is!' said Nosi Parka triumphantly. '*And* it's coming this way, *and* it's flying low! That means it'll settle somewhere near here for the night! And that's all I can tell you, my fine gentleman! *Good* evening!'

'Wait!' Abu Ali beseeched him. '*Please* tell me how Silver Bud is? Does she still have faith in me?'

'You're never out of her thoughts!' Nosi Parka assured him. 'But what a time to ask! Be off! The Land of Green Ginger won't come looking for *you*!'

'A thousand thanks and *away* we go!' cried Abu Ali gratefully, and rushed off into the forest.

'Hey!' cried Boomalakka Wee. 'Wait for me!' and he rushed off after Abu Ali.

'If they *think*,' exclaimed the mouse furiously, 'that they can get rid of me as easily as *that*, *my*, how wrong they are!' and she rushed off after Boomalakka Wee; and Nosi Parka was left sitting quietly in front of his cave stroking his nose, which was the largest in the world.

Abu Ali ran, and ran, and ran, and when he had run, and run, and run till he was out of breath, he reached the edge of the forest; and there stretched out before him was the Arabian Desert, looking very pink and yellow and flat and empty in the sunset; but though he strained his eyes and searched the sky from one end to the other, there was no sign of a blob that even remotely resembled the Land of Green Ginger looking for somewhere to settle for the night.

He sat down on a stone, and wished he had a drink of water after all that running; and soon he heard: '*Haphoo! Haphoo! Haphoo!*' and Boomalakka Wee emerged from the forest and fell wheezing to the ground beside him, too exhausted to speak, and a moment after *that* the mouse tripped out of the forest looking as cool as an igloo.

'No sign of it yet?' she inquired casually. 'I thought not. More haste, less speed!'

'I *won't* let the Land of Green Ginger slip through my fingers, now that I've got this far!' panted Abu Ali. 'As soon as I've got my breath back, I'm going to start running again!'

'By the time you get your breath back,' said the mouse practically, 'it will be dark. How will you know which way to run?'

'I don't know, but I'll keep on running!' said Abu Ali desperately. 'And I won't stop till I find the Land of Green Ginger!'

'Tut, rash lad; pause and consider!' the mouse advised him. 'Not one of us can see in the dark! We might easily run *away* from it, instead of *towards* it!

Besides and furthermore, if Boomalakka Wee took one more step, he'd burst!'

'I have! I am! I did!' groaned Boomalakka Wee dramatically. 'But never mind! Go on without me! . . . But, Abu Ali, promise me one thing; just *one* thing, Abu Ali? Tell them – tell them that I died with a smile on my lips? Will you tell them that, my loyal old comrade?'

'Oh, fudge,' said the mouse, entirely unimpressed, and that put a stop to *that*.

Chapter the Ninth

*Which Explains How Abu Ali Found the Button-Nosed
Tortoise and a Great Deal More Trouble As Well*

N ight had fallen over the Arabian Desert.

It was a particularly stark, dark, pitch black
night, and the air was cool and growing cooler every
minute, which meant that before long it would be
downright cold; and there sat Abu Ali, Boomalakka
Wee and the mouse, entirely surrounded by sand,
and Boomalakka Wee was shivering and blowing on
his fingers.

'If only the *moon* would come out!' said Abu Ali
desperately. 'For all we know, the Land of Green
Ginger may be somewhere near us at this very
moment!'

'Personally,' announced the mouse austerely,
sitting on her paws to keep them warm, 'I don't care
if it's flying upside-down and backwards, right above

our heads! I'm homesick, I miss my friends, and I'm *aching* for a scrap of toasted cheese!'

'Now, now; cheer up!' said Abu Ali kindly. 'Things are bound to get better!'

'Who cares if they do? They'll only get worse again!' returned the mouse, quite inconsolable, and two sedate tears rolled down her nose.

'You're not the only pebble on the beach!' said Boomalakka Wee pathetically. 'I'm homesick too!'

'*You* deserve to be!' the mouse informed him tensely. 'If it hadn't been for *you* –! Oh, I don't know why I bother! Water off a duck's back! Though I doubt that even a backward duck would answer a lamp it didn't know how to answer; and then start spells it didn't know how to finish –!'

She broke off suddenly, and patted the ground in a mystified manner with her paw.

'Abu Ali!' she said with all due caution. 'Something strange and peculiar is taking place!'

'What kind of something?' asked Abu Ali, straining his eyes in the dark.

'I don't know,' said the mouse, now openly alarmed.

'But it's taking place! I have an unaccountable conviction that I'm sitting on green grass!'

'That's just another bee in your bonnet!' said Boomalakka Wee with a regrettable lapse of manners.

Abu Ali patted the ground beside him, and instead of patting sand, he found he was patting green grass too.

'In that case, a bee's got into *my* bonnet as well!' he said. 'Because *I'm* sitting on green grass too! My, how quickly it must have grown!'

'And *now* I smell flowers!' announced the mouse.

'Sheer hallucinootions!' said Boomalakka Wee disrespectfully.

'No. I, too, smell flowers!' said Abu Ali. 'Is it possible that we've walked in our sleep? No, it can't be! We haven't been to sleep!'

'Then why are we no longer where we were, but elsewhere?' asked the mouse.

'We're not elsewhere!' said Boomalakka Wee. 'Because why? Because I don't smell any flowers, and I'm not sitting on green grass!'

But the brave words were no sooner out of his

mouth, when he gave vent to a sudden and heartfelt wail of alarm.

'Abu Ali ! I take it all back!' he cried remorsefully. 'Something strange and peculiar *has* taken place! I'm sitting on a stone, and there's running water all around me!'

'There he goes again, anything for attention!' said the mouse in deep disapproval. 'Pull yourself together, Wee! You've just been stung by a stray bee from one of our bonnets!'

'But I'm telling you the *truth*!' Boomalakka Wee insisted tearfully. 'That's why I'm so *cold*! It's a stone and I'm – I'm – *AH – H – H – CHOO!*'

His sneeze was followed by an enormous splash, then a bubbling noise, and then a very damp voice cried '*Glub – Glub – Ubble – Glug – Help!* I'm drowning.'

'What a *commotion*!' said the mouse primly. 'Anyone would think there was real water there!'

'There *is*!' insisted Boomalakka Wee in tears. 'I'm *in* it! – *Under* it – *Glub – Glub – Glub!*'

'Whereabouts are you?' shouted Abu Ali. 'Swim

towards me, and I'll help you out!'

'Unless you've sunk!' added the mouse practically.

'Boomalakka Wee! You haven't sunk, have you?' called Abu Ali anxiously.

The splashing came nearer.

'Yes. Twice!' answered Boomalakka Wee's voice dolefully, coming nearer still. 'But I can m-m-manage. It's not so deep *here* as it was *there*. But I'm frozen stiff!'

'If only the moon would come out!' said Abu Ali desperately. 'At least we could *see* what's happening!'

They heard Boomalakka Wee squelch on to dry land and begin to jump up and down, flapping his arms dispiritedly.

'A fine thing!' he remarked bitterly. 'You sit down on sand in the middle of the desert, and the next thing you know, you're up to your neck in ice-cold water! I'd like it explained, that's all!'

'It can only be another spell gone wrong,' the mouse decided ironically. 'You *do* attract them, Wee!'

'Look!' cried Abu Ali in relief. 'Here comes the moon at last!'

As he spoke a pale glow began stealing through the clouds, and as it brightened, they found themselves on the bank of a bubbling stream, in the middle of a delightful wood.

'It's a wood!' said Abu Ali immediately.

'So it is!' agreed the mouse. 'It's a wood!'

Boomalakka Wee stopped jumping up and down and looked about him.

'It's a w-w-wood,' he agreed heavily, 'and I'd like *that* explained, too!'

'Why, of course!' Abu Ali burst out excitedly. 'Why didn't we realize it at once? Boomalakka Wee! Mouse! *We're in the Land of Green Ginger!*'

'Who? Me?' asked Boomalakka Wee blankly.

'Prove it!' demanded the mouse.

'Nosi Parka *told* us it was going to settle somewhere for the night!' said Abu Ali. '*Well, we* were sitting on the particular piece of the Arabian Desert that it chose to settle on!'

'An interesting theory,' said the mouse. 'But if it settled *on* us, why aren't we *underneath* it instead of *in* it?'

'Ah,' said Abu Ali profoundly. 'Well, yes. But then again, why bother?'

'I heartily agree!' the mouse conceded. 'We have troubles enough!'

The moon was full and bright by now, and they could see the Land of Green Ginger quite clearly. It was sprinkled with ginger trees laden down with branch upon branch of sparkling sugar-coated green ginger, and big bright beauteous flowers grew all over the soft velvety grass, and water-lilies floated on the cheerful little hubble-bubbling stream. It was all charmingly rural and unspoilt and undisturbed by human hand. No bits of paper, no empty bottles, no initials carved on the tree-trunks. You cannot imagine such natural wonders, Gentle Reader; you must simply take my word for it.

'There's not a moment to be lost!' cried Abu Ali. 'We must find the magic Phoenix birds before the night's an hour older!'

'Not me!' announced Boomalakka Wee querulously. 'I'm staying right where I am! I've had enough! And I always spoil it for everyone else anyway!'

'Well, *you* said it; *I* didn't!' said the mouse, briskly. 'Lead on, Abu Ali! Good-bye, Wee!'

'Good-bye!' said Wee haughtily. 'And if I never see you again, I hope you run up a clock and never come down!'

But Abu Ali and the mouse had no sooner set off, when a loud whirring noise broke out directly above Boomalakka Wee's head, and he cried, 'Woo-*oo*! Wait for me!' and rushed after them.

'I thought you weren't coming?' said the mouse

with elaborate surprise, when he caught up with them.

'Some people can't take a joke!' said Boomalakka Wee hurriedly. 'Of *course* I'm coming with you! What do you suppose that noise was, Abu Ali?'

'What noise?' asked Abu Ali.

'That *Whirra – whirra – whirra?*'

And as he spoke, they all three heard the sound directly above them.

'Oh, dear. Don't tell me it's dragons,' said the mouse pessimistically.

Abu Ali gazed up at the tree-tops.

'No! Birds!' he said. '*Big* birds! It's the magic Phoenix birds! Two of them! Quickly, Boomalakka Wee; where's my bow and arrow? You were carrying it!'

'Was I?' asked Boomalakka Wee in a small voice.

Abu Ali turned around hastily.

'Of course you were! You *insisted* on carrying it! You haven't *lost* it?' he asked desperately.

'Well – not exactly lost it – the thing is – Don't be cross with me, Abu Ali – It's at the bottom of the stream,' said Boomalakka Wee dejectedly.

Without a word, Abu Ali caught him by the hand and rushed him back to the stream.

'Whereabouts did you fall in?' he asked quickly. 'Quick! Show me! Here?'

'No, there,' said Boomalakka Wee, pointing. 'No, wait a moment. Now I'm muddled. It was higher up. No; lower down.'

Abu Ali ran along the bank of the stream.

'Here?' he asked hurriedly.

'Yes,' said Boomalakka Wee, but without conviction.

Abu Ali jumped into the stream and began feeling about for the bow and arrow.

'Are you *sure* you fell in here?' he asked urgently.

Boomalakka Wee sat down on the bank and hugged his knees disconsolately.

'Not very,' he admitted forlornly. 'One part of a stream's much like another. It was near a rock.'

'The stream's *full* of rocks!' said the mouse briskly. 'Which rock?'

Abu Ali waded back up the steam till he was level with them.

'Which rock? *Try* to remember, Boomalakka Wee!' he beseeched.

'I *think* it was *that* one,' said Boomalakka Wee, pointing deparately at the first rock he saw.

Abu Ali splashed all around the rock.

'Find anything?' asked the mouse.

'Not a thing,' said Abu Ali.

'I didn't think you would,' said the mouse.

'It's all my fault!' admitted Boomalakka Wee, on the brink of tears. 'I *do* feel awful, Abu Ali!'

'Cheer up,' said Abu Ali. 'It may have drifted downstream. I'll look,' and he waded downstream until it turned a bend and they could see him no longer.

The mouse sat down beside Boomalakka Wee.

'Bravo. Fine Work! Good Old Wee!' she said scathingly. 'Always there in an emergency! Relax and leave it to Wee!'

'Madam,' said Boomalakka Wee, every inch a gentleman, 'the moment my spells *do* work, I'm going to conjure up a birthday present, just for *you*!'

'Oh, *are* you?' exclaimed the mouse, agreeably

surprised. 'What kind of present?'

'An enormous, hungry, marmalade tom-cat!' said Boomalakka Wee with intense feeling.

Abu Ali searched the stream till it disappeared under a rock, and at last decided that his bow and arrow was lost for ever.

He climbed wearily on to the bank, and began squeezing the water out of his clothes.

'My, my! You *are* wet, aren't you?' exclaimed a dignified but unfamiliar voice behind him.

Abu Ali jumped round quickly. A large tortoise was gazing at him inquiringly over a toadstool. It wore enormous spectacles at the end of its nose, which was shaped like a button.

'Why, it's *you*!' cried Abu Ali delightedly.

'It is indeed! And you must be Abu Ali?' replied the button-nosed tortoise with grave courtesy. 'I was beginning to fear we'd never meet! The odds against it were formidable – what with neither of us able to calculate where this erratic *flora and fauna cum laudibus* would decide to settle next! By the way, do those belong to you?' he added, waving his flipper at the bow and arrow, which lay on the bank. 'They came floating past a little while ago, and, having mistaken them for a rare variety of edible asparagus, I retrieved them!'

'I can never thank you enough!' vowed Abu Ali gratefully, picking up the bow and arrow. 'But first things first! How do I break your spell?'

'I can answer you in a nutshell,' the button-nosed tortoise assured him. 'Even without a nutshell. You observe that *large* water-lily (genus *oblata longata mompara)*, in the middle of the stream?'

'You mean, of course, the pink one?' said Abu Ali.

'I do indeed. Pick it, if you'd be so kind,' said the button-nosed tortoise. 'I'd have done it long ago, only I would have sunk. Can't swim,' he added scientifically. 'Once tried. Sank like a stone. Great handicap. Real tortoise swims like a bird. Correction. Fish. Watch out. Deep there. Deceptive!'

'Very!' agreed Abu Ali, once he had resurfaced and got the water out of his ears.

Carefully avoiding the deep hole, he picked the water-lily and waded back to the bank.

'Oh, well done! Well done!' cried the button-nosed tortoise cordially. 'Let me see it? Yes! That's the one!'

'Now what must I do?' asked Abu Ali.

'Now you hold it in your right hand; face the moon; and recite this slowly and carefully:

'Pi R-squared-sideways!
The Cube Root of Zero!
Manganese Potash
And Mushrooms on Toast!

172

Leaf of the Lily! And I, Abu Ali,
Turn you back into
The Man you Miss Most!'

'I don't promise to get it right the first time,' warned Abu Ali holding the water-lily in his right hand and facing the moon. 'But here we go! *Pi R-squared-sideways! The Cube Root of Zero!*' he repeated slowly and carefully. '*Manganese Potash and Mushrooms on Toast! Leaf of the Lily! And I, Abu Ali, Turn you back into the Man you Miss Most!*'

The button-nosed tortoise gave a gratified sigh of gorgeous relief.

'Did I do it right?' asked Abu Ali anxiously.

'Perfectly!' the button-nosed tortoise assured him.

'Then why are you still a button-nosed tortoise?' demanded Abu Ali in pardonable disappointment.

'The spell works in stages,' explained the button-nosed tortoise benignly. 'But the rest is child's play.' Whereupon he ate the water-lily. 'Tastes terrible,' he added, pulling a face, 'but at dawn tomorrow morning, I'll be myself again! Would you be kind enough to call on me just after sunrise?'

'Nothing would give me greater pleasure!' replied Abu Ali courteously.

'Thank you. Good evening,' returned the tortoise, and disappeared unexpectedly into his shell without another word.

Abu Ali hurried back to Boomalakka Wee and the mouse, who were sitting where he had left them.

'I found the button-nosed tortoise!' he cried in high excitement, 'and I've broken the spell – or shall have, by sunrise!'

'Something attempted, something done,' quoted the mouse with composure, 'Has earned a night's repose.'

'Oh, no, it hasn't!' said Abu Ali firmly. 'Not until I get my tail feathers from the Phoenix birds!'

'Oh, *them*!' said Boomalakka. Wee brightly. 'They flew away, quite some time ago!'

'Well, really, Boomalakka Wee! You could have kept an eye on them!' said Abu Ali with a touch of annoyance, and set off into the wood with his bow and arrow. The mouse pattered after him.

'Cheer up. They can't have gone far. It's not that

big a wood,' she said consolingly.

'Shh!' commanded Abu Ali, and they began tiptoeing silently along.

'*Yoo-hoo! Wait for mee-hee!*' yelled Boomalakka Wee in a voice so loud that its echoes met in the middle.

Abu Ali and the mouse jumped a foot in the air.

'*Quiet!*' hissed Abu Ali frantically.

'*Why!*' asked Boomalakka Wee, crushed.

'We're stalking Phoenix birds!' said the mouse severely. 'That is, we *were* before you bellowed the roof down!'

But even as she was speaking, they all heard the whirring sound above their heads again, and right above them were two magic Phoenix birds circling curiously, having mistaken Boomalakka Wee's voice for the mating call of a Zanzibar Ostrich.

What did the Phoenix birds look like, Gentle Reader? They looked like blue-and-purple storks, except that they had tufted golden crests on their heads, and emerald-green beaks and legs; and they sparkled and glittered in the moonlight like the precious stones in Aladdin's Cave.

Abu Ali drew his bow taut, aimed carefully, and *plunk-whissht!* his arrow shot into the air and neatly removed three tail feathers from the larger Phoenix bird.

It gave a shrill, startled screech, looped the loop, and then dived suddenly down towards them.

'Run!' squeaked the mouse. 'You've, *infuriated* him!'

She dived under a ginger bush, followed rapidly by Boomalakka Wee.

Abu Ali stood his ground, but he felt a little nervous when the Phoenix bird alighted in front of him, for it was *far* larger close-to than one would have imagined from a distance.

The Phoenix bird stood for a moment just glaring at Abu Ali dangerously; then he half closed one eye in a sinister way, and leaned forward till their heads were only separated by inches.

'Did *you* shoot out my tail feathers?' he asked grimly.

'Yes, sir,' said Abu Ali bravely. 'I did it with my bow and arrow.'

'On purpose?'

'I'm afraid, yes.'

'Things have come to a sad state,' said the Phoenix bird austerely, 'when a law-abiding, self-respecting Phoenix bird can't venture out of its nest without assault and battery to its tail feathers! Have we become a lawless nation?'

'It's an outrage!' said the second Phoenix bird shrilly, alighting beside her spouse. 'Sheer vandalism! Make an example of the dismal ruffian!'

'I'm not a dismal ruffian, ma'am!' Abu Ali assured her.

'But these three feathers are vitally necessary to me –'

'I like *that*!' squawked the Phoenix bird indignantly. 'I suppose they weren't vitally necessary to *me*? I suppose I'm to laugh it off? I suppose you think I can grow new tail feathers overnight? It's clear to the merest child that you've never undergone a moulting season!'

He shook with speechless fury for a moment, and then his curiosity got the better of him, and he added in a frankly inquisitive voice: '*Why* are they vitally necessary to you? You're not a bird!'

'I need them to win the hand of the jeweller's daughter, Silver Bud, whom I love with all my heart and soul!' said Abu Ali with impressive conviction.

'*Ho!*' said the lady Phoenix bird sharply. 'Then you *knew* they were valuable! That leaves you with no excuse whatsoever!'

'Oh, I wouldn't go so far as to say *that*, my dear,' said the first Phoenix bird in an unexpectedly amicable voice. 'Let us not be *too* hasty. After all, if the young gentleman needs them to win a bride, it hardly comes under the heading of vandalism. To the contrary, it's an indirect compliment. Suppose we consider it in that light, and say no more about it?'

'That's *exceedingly* generous of you, sir!' began Abu Ali gratefully; but the lady Phoenix bird wasn't letting him off as lightly as that.

'*If*,' she informed him haughtily, 'you had approached my husband in a polite and courteous manner, and not shot at him with a bow and arrow, we would willingly have *donated* three tail feathers left over from last season, and everyone would have been spared a very painful scene!'

'I agree, ma'am, I can only plead thoughtlessness and lack of consideration for others,' said Abu Ali humbly. 'I tender you my most profound apologies!'

'Pray don't give it another thought,' said the first Phoenix bird pleasantly. 'But if you come across any *other* young gentlemen who are after my tail feathers, you might explain that they don't have to use me for target practice, will you? As my wife says, we always have a few available. And I hope you win the jeweller's daughter! Come along, dear!'

And without more ado, the two Phoenix birds

spread their greeny-blue wings and flew up into the air and away.

Boomalakka Wee and the mouse crawled out from under the ginger bush and tried to look as if they hadn't been hiding there.

'That bird could give a number of people I know a lesson in dignity and good manners,' said the mouse, profoundly impressed.

'He could indeed!' agreed Abu Ali, picking up the three tail feathers with loving care. 'Now! First we'll snatch a little sleep; and tomorrow morning, as soon as I've made sure the spell worked on the magician, we start on the journey back to Samarkand!'

But, alas, Gentle Reader, what no one suspected at the moment, was that the wicked princes, and Abu Ali, and the Land of Green Ginger, although they had started from three separate directions, all had the same destination in common; and *you* know, and *I* know that this can have only one result.

Whether they liked it or not, eventually they were all bound to meet.

Chapter the Tenth

*Which Explains How the Wicked Princes Went Back to
Their Old Tricks Again*

*T*he wicked Princes Tintac Ping Foo and Rubdub Ben
Thud were utterly exhausted. They had been
carrying the magic carpet across the Arabian Desert
for a whole day, and neither of them was used to
carrying *anything*, let alone a magic carpet that grew
steadily heavier and heavier as they plodded along.

Small Slave was his usual resourceful self, however.

He composed a marching song for the retinues to sing, to bolster their masters' morale.

It went:

What lies twixt We and Samarkand?
Nothing but Sand, and Sand, and Sand,
And Sand, and Sand, and only Sand!
A Sandy Road we could understand,
But how can we follow the Lay of a Land
Where the Sand's all Road,
And the Road's all Sand,
And every Horizon we have scanned
Is as Flat as the Back
Of a Flat Man's Hand?
We'd ever so rather go by Boat –
Even a Boat that Don't Much Float –
The Trouble with Deserts; which Gets our Goat;
Is the Sand, Sand, Sand!
No wonder the Sphinx has lost her Nose!
And What Keeps Adding to all her Woes?
We don't know much, but this we knows!
It's Sand, Sand, Sand!

If you can imagine this sung in part-harmony, Gentle Reader; supported by Rubdub Ben Thud singing: *'Kadoo, kadunk, kadee; kadoodle-oodle-skippety-wee!'* in contrapuntal semi-quavers, you'll know how endless that journey felt, and how everyone was longing for it to be over.

Small wonder, then, that when they saw the Land of Green Ginger in the distance, they were almost hysterical with relief.

'Look! Look!' cried Rubdub Ben Thud. 'An oasis! Head for it, Small Slave!'

'We must be off our route!' said Small Slave, puzzled. 'It wasn't here the last time we passed!'

'Nonsense!' snapped Rubdub. 'I remember it *perfectly*!'

He looked over his shoulder at the wicked Prince Tintac Ping Foo.

'I suppose *you'll* think it's just a trick to steal the carpet, if I suggest we rest here for the night?' he asked coldly.

'No,' returned Ping Foo smugly, 'because I shall rest on *my* half of the carpet!'

'You *would*!' muttered Rubdub under his breath. 'A suspicious mind, and not much of it!'

'Would you care to repeat that without a potato in your mouth?' asked Ping Foo superciliously.

'Certainly!' Rubdub cried willingly. 'I'll be glad to add this too! If you *weren't* a man with a suspicious mind and not much of it, we wouldn't be carrying this carpet half-way round the world!'

'I quite agree!' sneered Ping Foo. 'You'd have stolen it!

By this time the caravans of the wicked princes had reached the edge of the Land of Green Ginger, and Small Slave, who had hurried on ahead to find a good place to pitch their camp, now came running back out of the trees excitedly.

'Stop!' he hissed to the wicked princes. 'Don't advance another *inch*!'

'Why not?' asked Rubdub nervously. 'Robbers? Dragons? Bogeymen?'

'No! your rival, Abu Ali!' returned Small Slave rapidly. 'He's here before you! Asleep! And he's no longer alone! He has accomplices with him – a small green man and a mouse! Both asleep also! Fate has delivered them into our hands, Master! He must never be allowed to reach Samarkand alive, or he'll win Silver Bud! There's nothing for it but!'

'What shockingly bad grammar!' exclaimed Ping Foo disapprovingly.

'Why is it shockingly bad grammar?' challenged Rubdub.

'Because a sentence without syntax is like an egg without salt!' said Ping Foo.

Rubdub's face went red.

'There you go again, dragging in eggs!' he said fiercely. 'You *know* I hate the very mention of the word!'

'I was referring solely to Small Slave's grammar!' said Ping Foo irritably.

'Overlook my grammar for the moment!' begged Small Slave urgently. 'If you want to remove your rival for ever from your path, you must act, and act *now*! Put down the carpet a moment, and come and look!'

'I don't let go of this carpet,' said Ping Foo

resolutely. 'Not for a *second*!'

'Nor me!' said Rubdub Ben Thud. 'Not for all the chee in Tina!'

'Then bring it with you!' exhorted Small Slave impatiently. 'But we *must* strike while the iron's hot! Ho, there, guards!' he hissed efficiently. 'Bring some rope!'

'How much rope?' asked the Head Guard vaguely. 'A lot?'

'Enough to tie up one and a half men; and enough string to tie up a mouse! This way, Masters!' he added to the two wicked princes. 'And don't make a *sound*, or we'll have counted our chickens before they're hatched!'

'Here we go with eggs again!' said Rubdub through his teeth.

'*Hush!*' said Small Slave.

'*Hush!*' said Ping Foo.

'*Hush yourselves!*' said Rubdub smouldering.

The three of them tiptoed cautiously through the ginger trees, followed by the guards with the rope and the piece of string, until they came to the clearing where Abu Ali and Boomalakka Wee and the mouse were peacefully asleep.

'There!' hissed Small Slave. 'What did I tell you? *Still on tiptoe, guards! – By the right, forward march! – Bind them!*'

'And mind the knots are tight!' added Rubdub Ben Thud, nervously retreating a little in case the wrong side won.

The guards crept up on the unsuspecting trio, and before Abu Ali and Boomalakka Wee and the mouse were properly awake, they had been overpowered and bound hand and foot; and to add insult to injury, Small Slave tore three strips off Boomalakka Wee's turban and gagged them.

As soon as they were sure that neither Abu Ali nor Boomalakka Wee nor the mouse could move or make a sound, the wicked princes swaggered up boldly and laughed in their faces.

'That'll teach you, Abu Ali!' jeered Tintac Ping Foo triumphantly. 'That'll make you rue the day you dared to cross our paths!'

'We'll remember you to Silver Bud!' Rubdub Ben Thud assured them sarcastically. 'By the by, do you notice what we're carrying? It's our magic egg – I mean, our magic carpet! – and we're on our way to Samarkand! We *do* wish you were coming with us; oh, we do, we do! Drop us a line when you're not so tied up! Well, we must be going! Good-bye, uncouth upstart!'

'Wait!' said Small Slave quickly. 'We can find good use for these magic feathers too!'

'Ah yes!' said Tintac Ping Foo quickly. 'Give them to me, Small Slave! I'll look after them!'

'Oh, no you don't!' cried Rubdub in a flash. 'Not on your egg – I mean, not on your life, Ping Foo! – Small Slave found them, and Small Slave shall keep them until we reach Samarkand!'

The wicked Prince Tintac Ping Foo, though greatly tempted, restrained a wild desire to hit Rubdub with the carpet, and shrugged his shoulders.

'Very well,' he said, pretending not to care. 'We haven't time to argue about omelettes – I mean, trifles! Which is the way out of here?'

'This way,' said Small Slave. 'And if I may make the suggestion, it would be wiser for your Highnesses to ride the rest of the way by camel, as time is now precious!'

'*I don't let go this carpet –!*' began Tintac Ping Foo and Rubdub Ben Thud in the same indignant breath.

'You don't need to!' Small Slave assured them soothingly. 'If you spread the carpet over one of the hardier camels, you can *both* ride on top of it, thereby killing two birds with one egg – I mean *stone!*'

'There's no getting away from it,' said Rubdub admiringly. 'You have to admit it. Small Slave has a brilliant egg – I mean *brain*!'

Abu Ali struggled with all his might, but the ropes had been too expertly tied, and he was unable to move or even cry out. When he saw the wicked princes depart, taking the magic Phoenix bird's feathers with them, it needed all his fortitude to ward off black despair; for at the moment, there seemed no hope whatsoever of reaching Samarkand in time to rescue Silver Bud; which meant, of course, that she was as good as lost.

This is what is known in the more refined literary circles as a terrible predicament, Gentle Reader, and I shall pause long enough for you to weigh with impunity the implausibility of its inimicably imponderable implications.

By dawn the next day, the wicked princes had ridden at such a gallop all through the night that they were almost half-way to Samarkand.

They would have been even nearer, except that they were so *exorbitantly* heavy, when added together, that they had to keep changing camels, and this wasted many precious hours.

When the sun rose, it occurred to Abu Ali, as he lay trussed and helpless, that the button-nosed tortoise's spell should have been broken by now. This being so, sheer gratitude, (if nothing else), should inspire the magician to come looking for him.

The hours crept by, however, and the magician *didn't* come looking for him, so at last Abu Ali had no choice but to presume that the spell hadn't been broken after all, and that no help could be expected from that quarter or any other.

He wriggled over on his side and looked for hopeful signs from Boomalakka Wee and the mouse. Boomalakka Wee showed none, mainly because he had gone to sleep from sheer exasperation; but the mouse, who was made of sterner stuff, was busy nibbling the piece of turban that Small Slave had tied around her nose, and had almost nibbled it through, for she had been working on it all night long.

Indeed, as Abu Ali watched, the noble rodent freed her nose, and then began, with one swift squeak of triumph, on the string which bound her paws together; mere child's play. When she was completely

free, she scampered over to Abu Ali and set about nibbling the rope round his hands.

Now this was a formidable task for any mouse, for the rope was not only thick and strong, but had been tarred, and tar had *particularly* painful associations for the mouse, because it recalled to mind a friend who had run away to sea and never come back, though she still nursed hopes of a letter of apology from him.

At last, however, the rope was nibbled right through, and as soon as he was free, Abu Ali swept her up in his arms and kissed her on both cheeks.

'Fie!' she protested. 'How ostentatious!' but she blushed delightedly none the less, for no one had kissed her since the friend had run away to sea, which was many years before.

Boomalakka Wee, as soon as Abu Ali released him, sat up with a look of battle in his eye and said: 'Just let me at 'em, that's all! Just let me lay my hands on that Tintac Pong Thump!'

'We have to overtake them first!' returned Abu Ali quickly. 'And they're a *long* way off by now! Quick! Follow me!'

With this, he flung himself along the path the wicked princes had taken the night before. Boomalakka Wee had gone two short steps in pursuit when he suddenly shouted: '*Ouch!*' and then: '*Wouch!*' and wobbled to the ground in a heap.

The mouse, against her better judgement, turned round and ran back to him.

'Really, what a fusspot you are!' she rallied him urgently. 'Back on your toes, Wee; or you'll get left behind again!'

'I can't! It's my legs!' wailed Boomalakka Wee. 'They've gone numb through being tied up so long! I can't *move*, mouse!'

The next moment Abu Ali came racing back into the clearing.

'Things have gone from bad to worse!' he cried in understandable despair. 'Now we'll *never* get out of here!'

'Of *course* we will! Why ever not?' cried the mouse, much disconcerted.

'Because we're miles up in the air!' cried Abu Ali. 'The Land of Green Ginger's off again, *and its going the wrong way*!'

Chapter the Eleventh

Which Explains How Sulkpot Ben Nagnag Went Back On His Word

*F*or a moment no one spoke because of the awful blow it was to be miles up in the air *and* going the wrong way. Then the mouse broke the silence.

'Well, there's no hurry about getting up, then, Wee,' she said, adding conversationally to Abu Ali: 'Wee's legs have rather let him down.'

'But, Abu Ali!' exclaimed Boomalakka Wee, not meeting the crisis with the same fortitude as the mouse. 'There *must* be *some* way of stopping it!'

'None!' said Abu Ali. 'We're helpless until it decides to land again! If *only* the spell had worked on the button-nosed tortoise! Well; the least I can do is go and look for him! He may be able to think of *something* we can do!'

'Wait for me!' said the mouse instantly. 'I *hate* to

feel I'm missing something!'

She trotted after Abu Ali, leaving a mournful Boomalakka Wee patting himself all over very tenderly and wishing with all his might, for the seventy-seven-thousandth time since yesterday, that he had thought twice about answering the lamp when Abu Ali rubbed it.

Abu Ali and the mouse followed the stream round the bend, and come to the clearing where he had left the button-nosed tortoise the night before.

There was not the slightest trace of a button-nosed tortoise to be seen; but what they *did* see was a

scholarly old gentleman with white whiskers, wearing a dignified robe and making notes in a big leather notebook.

'Who are you? Stowaways?' he inquired in surprise, peering at them over his enormous spectacles. 'Why; bless my wand and whiskers; it's Abu Ali! What a welcome sight! When you didn't appear this morning, I assumed you'd left for parts unknown on pressing business!'

'Then the spell *did* work!' cried Abu Ali in delight, and at once informed the magician of the awful treachery of the wicked Princes Tintac Ping Foo and Rubdub Ben Thud, and how urgent it was for him to reach Samarkand while there was still time to save Silver Bud; concluding with an earnest request to the magician to let them out at the next stop.

'The next stop?' echoed the Magician. 'Bless my wand and whiskers, I'll do more than that! I'll take you right to Samarkand!'

And he was as good as his word, for he had no sooner made one or two small magic passes in the air, when the Land of Green Ginger slowed down, banked smoothly, and began flying back the way it had come.

'You see?' chirped the magician delightedly. 'It's working *perfectly*! And bless my wand and whiskers if I haven't forgotten to thank you for breaking my spell! What an absent-minded, unappreciative old codger I am! You're a fine young lad; and whatever service I can do for you in return is as good as done! Ask anything – anything!' he added encouragingly.

The mouse tugged at Abu Ali's slipper.

'Ask him to turn those wicked princes into beetles!' she whispered longingly. 'Then *all* our troubles are at an end!'

'Beetles? Nothing easier!' the magician assured Abu Ali willingly. 'You have but to say the word!'

Abu Ali pondered this for a moment, for in many ways, it was a tempting offer. But at last he shook his head.

'No,' he decided, with only slight reluctance. 'Two wrongs don't make a right. Besides, I shouldn't be able to kick Rubdub Ben Thud, if he were a beetle; and I've been saving it up for a *long* time now!

Furthermore, think how miserable they'd make life for all the other beetles! No,' he said resolutely, 'they must be beaten by fair means! I'd sooner you helped Boomalakka Wee and the mouse. They're extremely anxious to return home; but Boomalakka Wee's spells aren't all they should be, and they can't get back. Could you kindly assist them?'

'Well, before I start anything, I'd have to familiarize myself with the type of spell they're under!' replied the magician cautiously, 'because once one makes a slip, *Poof!* – and one's a button-nosed tortoise, for instance; like I was, for instance; waiting nineteen years for you to grow up and break the spell! But hark at me chattering away when duty calls! Where is this Boomalakka Wee?'

'Just round the corner and on a bit,' said Abu Ali, and they all went back to where Boomalakka Wee was still patting himself soothingly all over, and introduced him to the magician.

Both of them at once plunged into a long and complicated discussion about spells, in the course of which it became steadily more obvious to Boomalakka

Wee that he knew even less about the magic lamp and what worked it than he thought he did, which had never been much.

All this time, the mouse was strangely quiet and subdued for a mouse who was about to be restored to her friends at long last; for she showed no interest whatsoever in the long and complicated discussion between Boomalakka Wee and the magician, which had now become so highly complicated that it was *miles* over Boomalakka Wee's head.

At last, however, the magician held up his hand and nodded sagely and said: 'I think, without presumption, that I have diagnosed the fundamental miscalculation! Without doubt this is a case of a clogged spell!'

'You mean you can unclog it?' chittered Boomalakka Wee, hardly daring to believe his ears.

'We are still in the experimental stage, and must not run before we can walk,' replied the magician carefully, 'so I propose that we examine the problem step by step. Now the proper procedure for returning djinns of the lamp to their correct postal address, I gather, is for them to stamp on the ground, which forthwith opens and swallows them. Am I correct so far?

'Yes, your Honour! Whatever you say, your Honour!' said Boomalakka Wee humbly, not having understood a *word*.

'So far, so good. Now kindly stamp on the ground,' requested the magician, 'and let me watch for possible errors.'

'I'm afraid his legs are too numb,' began the mouse.

'Not now they're not!' cried Boomalakka Wee excitedly, and stamped hard. 'Look! This is the way I stamped, which is *exactly* how father always did it; but nothing happens, see? *Nothing!*'

He stamped twice more to remove all doubt.

The magician closed one eye and concentrated with formidable concentration, and there was absolute quiet in the Land of Green Ginger, except for the soft *swoosh-swoosh* it made as it sailed through the air.

At last the magician opened his eye and smiled a wise and scientific smile.

'*Eureka!*' he announced proudly.

'*Eureka?*' repeated Boomalakka Wee bewilderedly.

'He means he's solved it!' explained Abu Ali.

'*S-s-solved it?*' echoed Boomalakka Wee, not daring to believe his ears. '*H-h-h-how?*'

'Elementary, my dear Wee,' said the magician airily, and having paused long enough to achieve the maximum dramatic effect, he added solemnly: 'You have been stamping with the wrong foot!'

'The wrong –' chittered Boomalakka Wee, and then gulped. 'The wrong f-f-f–' and had to stop and gulp again, because his ears were now singing like crickets. '*The wrong foot –?*'

'That's right,' said the magician kindly. 'The wrong foot. Now try stamping with the other one!'

Without another word (for he could think of none sufficiently auspicious), Boomalakka Wee stamped with his other foot with all his might, then clapped his hands over his eyes because he could hardly bear to look; but his fears were groundless, for his other foot had barely touched the ground when there was a rumble of thunder that made everybody jump, and the ground split open right under their noses.

Before the mouse could blink, Boomalakka Wee was turning into a small, blissful green cloud.

'Oh, joy! Good-bye! Good-bye!' he cried in a transport of delight.

'Wee, come back!' called Abu Ali anxiously. 'You're forgetting the mouse!'

'My goodness, so I am!' exclaimed the green cloud apologetically, turning back into Boomalakka Wee. 'Come along, mouse!'

But to everyone's surprise, the mouse unexpectedly shook her head.

'No, thank you, Wee,' she replied calmly. 'I've changed my mind.'

'What?' asked Boomalakka Wee, amazed. 'You mean you're not coming back with me?'

'I have already expressed myself to that effect!' said the mouse.

'Come, come, madam,' warned the magician. 'That means you may *never* be able to get back!'

'Doubtless,' shrugged the mouse.

'But what can have changed your mind, at the very last minute?' demanded Abu Ali. 'You've been eating your little heart out to get home!'

'When a lady chooses to change her mind,' said the mouse with a touch of hauteur, 'a gentleman would consider it no more than her privilege, and not badger her about it. But if you *must* know,' she added, 'it's because I should never know a *moment's* peace, if I left while things were still at sixes and sevens! I *must* know what happens in the end, if it costs me my whiskers!'

'Your fortitude and your courage leave me speechless with admiration,' Abu Ali told her gallantly. 'But I beg you to reconsider your decision, ma'am, if only for the sake of the friends who have become anxious!'

'I said no and I meant no!' said the mouse. 'Don't let us keep you, Wee!'

But Boomalakka Wee was gazing at the mouse as if he had been rapped smartly on his little green head by a falling coconut.

'I have never in my life felt so stupid!' he burst out remorsefully. '*Or* so thoughtless! *Or* so selfish! Pardon me while I kick myself!'

He did so, hard.

'What ever was *that* for?' asked the mouse in surprise.

'For thinking only of my silly self in the excitement of the moment!' he said. 'You *just* brought me to my senses in the nick of time, mouse!'

'Don't tell me *you've* decided not to go home either?' demanded the mouse. 'Really! Of all the copycats! Shoo! Be off with you!'

'Of *course* I won't go home till we all know what happens in the end!' vowed Boomalakka Wee resolutely. 'Why, what a fair weather friend I'd be! I'd never be able to look myself in the eye again! And quite apart from everything else, Abu Ali, how *ever* would you manage without me?'

'Abu Ali,' observed the magician, profoundly impressed, 'you are indeed fortunate in possessing two such loyal companions! Few there are, who would not envy you, egad!'

'I can only assure you, mouse; *and* you, Boomalakka Wee,' said Abu Ali simply, 'that you have touched me far more deeply than I can ever tell you!'

'Oh, pish!' said the mouse with a blush. 'Let's not make mountains out of cheese-crumbs!'

And as she spoke, the Land of Green Ginger began to tip gently to one side.

'Please take your seats! We're landing!' called the magician excitedly. 'Doesn't she do it *beautifully*?'

They all seated themselves until a soft bump in formed them that the Land of Green Ginger had come to rest. Then they stood up and proceeded together to the edge of the wood.

So accurate was the Land of Green Ginger's sense of direction, Gentle Reader, that there, directly facing them, were the gates of Samarkand. And sitting on the ground in front of the gates, gazing in stunned stupefication at the Land of Green Ginger, was Omar Khayyam.

'Why, if it isn't Omar Khayyam! I'm back!' cried Abu Ali, but Omar Khayyam was unable to remove his gaze from the Land of Green Ginger.

'Abu Ali,' he requested in subdued, uneasy tones, 'Would you be kind enough to pinch me?'

Abu Ali obliged, and he shook his head.

'Oh, that's bad!' he said with profound misgiving. 'It's still there! Only a moment ago, Abu Ali, I was sitting here without a care in the world – so I thought! – composing a verse about the wilderness being pawadise enough, if I had a jug of wine, a book of verse and thou – meaning a young lady I sold a tent to yesterday – when all of a sudden – *pff!* One moment, wilderness; the next, botanical gardens! That isn't wight, you know. Would you *be* kind enough to inform me whether *you* see wilderness – which it ought to be! – or botanical whatnot, which it *oughtn't!*'

'You're looking at the one-and-only, large-as-life-and-twice-as-natural Land of Green Ginger!' Abu Ali reassured him proudly. 'May I present to you the illustrious magician who made it? And my two faithful companions, Madam Mouse and the Genie Boomalakka Wee?'

'How dee doo?' said the magician.

'How dee doo?' said the mouse.

'How dee doo?' said Boomalakka Wee.

'So you're *not* an optical illusion!' said Omar Khayyam in vast relief, scrambling to his feet and bowing. 'Allow me to say that I'm delighted to make your acquaintances! But where are the three tail fevvers? And what happened to the wicked pwinces?'

Whereupon everyone explained everything to everyone else's satisfaction; and then the magician said regretfully: 'Well, Abu Ali, my friend and benefactor, if I don't want to cause trouble by obstructing a public thoroughfare, I'll have to be off. Are you *certain* you don't want me to turn the wicked princes into beetles?'

'No indeed, sir!' Abu Ali replied. 'You've been

more than obliging as it is!'

On this cordial note the magician said good-bye all round, re-entered the Land of Green Ginger, and turned its foliaged prow towards the sky.

Abu Ali and Omar Khayyam and the mouse and Boomalakka Wee stood and watched it ascend gracefully and disappear into the clouds.

At the very moment that it disappeared from sight, the mouse slapped her forehead in vexation.

'You know what we forgot to do?' she demanded of the other. 'We forgot to ask the Phoenix birds for three more tail feathers!'

'Now, why couldn't you have thought of that while there was still time?' asked Boomalakka Wee severely.

'Why couldn't *you*?' returned the mouse.

'Why couldn't *I*?' said Abu Ali, shouldering the blame. 'Still, there is no time to cry over spilt milk! I must now present myself before Sulkpot Ben Nagnag, and supply him with an exact account of everything that has happened.'

'*Without* the three tail feathers?' asked the mouse.

'*Without* the three tail feathers!' nodded Abu Ali.

'Wouldn't it be safer to wite him a letter?' suggested Omar Khayyam.

'Perhaps,' said Abu Ali. 'But what conviction would it carry? None! No, no; he must be bearded in his den!'

'Our fwiend Abu Ali is a stubborn fellow,' said Omar Khayyam with misgiving to the mouse.

'He has a will of iron!' agreed the mouse loyally.

Whereupon they entered Samarkand and proceeded briskly to the house of Sulkpot Ben Nagnag.

When they reached the gate, Abu Ali turned to the other three and said: 'Well, my friends, here we part company for the time being.'

'Aren't we coming in with you?' asked the mouse, dismayed.

'No,' said Abu Ali kindly. 'You two go with Omar Khayyam, and wait for me at his tent shop.'

'But I hardly know him!' protested the mouse. 'And for all I know, he may keep a cat!'

'You may wely on me to pwotect you from *all* hostile twibes, now and at any time, ma'am!' Omar Khayyam reassured her gallantly.

'Why, thank you!' said the mouse, but added to Abu Ali, 'All the same, I shan't have a moment's peace till I know you're safe!'

'Me neither!' agreed Boomalakka Wee unhappily.

'If all goes well, I'll send word to you within the hour,' Abu Ali promised them, knocking on the gate.

'And if all *doesn't* go well?' asked the mouse.

'Never trouble trouble till trouble troubles *you*!' said Abu Ali. 'But just for safe-keeping,' he added, handing the lamp to Omar Khayyam, 'I'll leave this in your care.'

'It couldn't be in safer hands,' Omar Khayyam assured him, slipping it absent-mindedly into his pocket.

At this moment, the gate opened.

'Oh, it's *you*, is it?' exclaimed the gateman, recognizing Abu Ali at once. 'Come *in*, my fine young gent! Come in! Sulkpot Ben Nagnag will be tickled *pink* to see *you*!'

Abu Ali stepped inside, and the guard slammed the gate behind him and locked it.

Omar Khayyam shook his head.

'That was *not* a hewo's welcome!' he said uneasily. 'I don't like it at *all*!'

'Me neither!' said Boomalakka Wee.

'I *knew* we should have gone with him!' said the mouse in bitter self-reproach.

'Well, all we can do now is wait and see,' said Omar Khayyam. 'Would you care to wide home in my hat, ma'am?'

'Good heavens, why? I have four perfectly good legs!' replied the mouse sedately.

When the guard had slammed the gate and locked it, he led Abu Ali to a courtyard where the Captain of the Guard and Kublai Snoo were playing darts in a corner. When they saw Abu Ali, they gazed at him with open mouths, then quickly drew their swords.

'You don't mean to say you've come *back*?' demanded the Captain of the Guard incredulously. 'Why, you must be out of your *mind*, young fellamelad!'

'Yes, indeed!' agreed Kublai Snoo. '*You* didn't know when you were lucky!'

'I wish to see Sulkpot Ben Nagnag, gentlemen,' Abu Ali requested politely. 'Will you inform him of my presence here?'

'That's *exactly* what we're going to do; and you're going to come along and watch us!' said the Captain of the Guard, putting the point of his sword into Abu Ali's ribs and leading him into the house. 'Upon my word, I feel downright sorry for you!'

'I do too!' agreed Kublai Snoo.

'Why?' asked Abu Ali.

'Because old Nagnag hates you to pieces, cross my heart and hope to die!' said Kublai Snoo, running to keep up. 'He does, doesn't he, Captain of the Guard?'

'That's for us to know, and him to find out!' said the Captain of the Guard ominously, and opened a door. 'In you go!'

In Abu Ali went, and there was Sulkpot Ben Nagnag lolling on a couch with his slippers off, doing a little wire puzzle; and when he saw Abu Ali, he dropped the little wire puzzle and sat bolt upright.

'WHAT? YOU AGAIN?' he shouted in capital letters, leaping to his feet, and shuffling into his slippers. 'My eyes deceive me! How *dare* you show your face here again? Off to the oil vats with him! Wait a moment! What in the name of grumbling thunder induced you to come back here, you brazen-faced insect? Explain yourself! Explain yourself INSTANTLY!'

'That, sir, is my intention!' Abu Ali informed him courteously. 'I found the three tail feathers of the magic Phoenix bird; and in view of the fact that the wicked princes could only find *one* magic carpet, I hereby and forthwith claim the hand of your daughter Silver Bud in marriage!'

'You – *what?*' gasped Sulkpot, unutterably beside himself. 'You – you – you – *what?* I shall choke or something! Water, water! You have the *insolence* – you have the *audacity* – you have the *arrogance* to ask for the hand of my – of my –!'

Here he *did* choke, and had to sit down hurriedly on the couch.

'Didn't I tell one of you dummies to bring me a drink of water?' he added hoarsely to the captain and Kublai Snoo. 'Don't gape at me! I did! Where is it? What do I pay you for? By the beard of my grandmother! Are my own soldiers defying me now?'

'We can't leave the prisoner to go running off after glasses of water,' said the Captain of the Guard sulkily. 'He'd escape or something.'

'No, he wouldn't,' said Kublai Snoo unexpectedly.

'Yes, he would,' said the captain quickly.

'Oh, no, he wouldn't,' said Kublai Snoo with quiet calm.

'Oh, yes, he would,' said the captain sharply.

'He wouldn't!' said Kublai Snoo swiftly.

'He *would*!' returned the captain, fiercely.

'SILENCE!' roared Sulkpot Ben Nagnag, then drew a long deep breath and made an effort to pull himself together. 'Now,' he said in a steadier voice, 'we'll deal with the situation in a cool, calm, and collected manner; if it's all the same to everybody! You, creature! You say you have the three tail feathers from the magic Phoenix bird?'

'I do,' said Abu Ali.

'Then produce them!' barked Sulkpot.

'He *would* have escaped,' muttered the captain under his breath.

'Oh, no, he wouldn't!' murmured Kublai Snoo quick as a flash.

'And I say he would!' mumbled the captain stubbornly.

'WILL YOU BE QUIET?' roared Sulkpot, turning purple. 'Do you understand me? Was I loud enough? BE QUIET!' He regained his breath with considerable difficulty, and turned to Abu Ali. 'I'm asking for the three tail feathers!' he said darkly. 'Produce them!'

'I can't yet!' said Abu Ali. 'They were stolen from me by the wicked princes, so we'll both have to wait till they get here.'

'You must take me for a doddering old idiot if you expect me to believe *that*!' snarled Sulkpot.

'I most certainly do!' Abu Ali assured him with spirit.

'What? Take me for a doddering old idiot?' exploded Sulkpot.

'No. I most certainly expect you to believe it!' said Abu Ali.

'*Would!*' said the captain inaudibly.

'*Wouldn't!*' said Kublai Snoo out of the corner of his mouth.

'*Would!*'

'*Wouldn't!*'

'*Look!*' said Sulkpot in an alarmingly hoarse whisper. 'The next sound *either* of you makes, you'll both go straight into the oil vat; armour and all! Is that absolutely clear? Did it sink in? Or don't you believe I meant it?'

'Yes,' said the Captain of the Guard.

'No,' said Kublai Snoo.

'WHAT?' roared Nagnag, clutching at the couch.

'He can't throw us in the oil vat,' said Kublai Snoo to the captain serenely. 'It's our Thursday afternoon off in a minute. We caught a suitor!'

'So we did! Where are you going?' asked the Captain of the Guard interestedly.

'Oh, just up and down the town,' said Kublai Snoo airily. 'Just looking about, and talking to people.'

'Would you mind if I came with you?' asked the captain, charmed by the idea.

'Yes, if you like,' said Kublai Snoo generously. 'Have you any money?'

'A little,' admitted the captain cautiously.

'Then we might go for a camel ride or something,' said Kublai Snoo. 'You can get a special return ticket which works out *very* reasonable.'

Abu Ali nudged them both, which was easy enough to do, as they were chatting across him.

'I think you're forgetting where you are,' he reminded them; and the Captain of the Guard and Kublai Snoo jumped hastily to attention and saluted.

Sulkpot Ben Nagnag, who had been sitting on the couch significantly tapping one foot, coughed.

'Quite finished?' he asked.

'Yes, thank you,' said the Captain.

'I *can* get a word in edgeways now?' inquired Sulkpot, deceptively polite.

'Yes, indeed!' said Kublai Snoo generously.

'*Thank* you!' said Sulkpot with heavy sarcasm.

'Thank *you*,' returned Kublai Snoo, bowing. 'And I'd like to add that I've always been very happy here. Very happy.'

'Me too,' said the Captain of the Guard appreciatively.

'May *I* be allowed a word, gentlemen?' asked Abu Ali, hoping to avert a regrettable scene.

'Be my guest!' said the captain hospitably.

'The floor is yours!' Kublai Snoo added generously.

'Thank you,' said Abu Ali, and addressed himself to Sulkpot. 'Permit me to remind you, sir, that I am a guest in your house,' he said with dignity. 'I came here in good faith. I have told you the truth. The least I am entitled to, in return, is a fair hearing!'

'My, you *are* brave!' said Kublai Snoo admiringly.

'Don't worry! You'll get it!' smouldered Sulkpot.

'When?' insisted Abu Ali.

'As soon as the princes arrive!' said Sulkpot. 'They will be used as evidence against you! Lock up this insect in solitary confinement till the princes arrive!'

'Is he allowed visitors?' asked the captain.

'NO, YOU MUTTON HEAD, OF COURSE NOT!' yelled Sulkpot.

'Well; we were only asking,' said Kublai Snoo sensitively. 'Why are you always such a pig to us?'

Sulkpot drew himself to his full height.

'Both guards! One pace forward march!' he ordered.

Kublai Snoo and the captain beamed and marched one pace forward smartly, expecting promotion or at least a medal.

Sulkpot stretched out both his arms and banged their helmets together.

'*Ouch!*' cried the captain.

'*Clang!*' cried Kublai Snoo.

'Now mark my every word!' said Sulkpot through clenched teeth. 'If the prisoner escapes before he is brought to trial, I'll boil all *three* of you in oil! Did *that* sink in?'

'Oh, *yessir*!' said the captain earnestly.

'It's still sinking!' Kublai Snoo assured him.

'Then bind the knave!' roared Sulkpot.

The captain and Kublai Snoo clapped hand-irons on to Abu Ali's wrists.

'Now to the dungeons with him!' shouted Sulkpot.

'Yes, sir! Right away, sir!' said the captain. 'Prisoner! About face! Eyes right! Number off!'

'One moment!' cried Abu Ali with admirable restraint. 'I see now how rash I was to trust you and expect fair play! But as I *still* wish to prove myself worthy of Silver Bud on my own merits alone, I advise you for *your* sake not to bring about my untimely end *unless* you invite the Emperor of China to attend it!'

'Well, I may not be able to manage *that*,' said Sulkpot sarcastically, 'but I'll send him a postcard afterwards! Away with him, guards!'

Thus were the mouse's profoundest misgivings fulfilled.

Abu Ali was marched to the nether-most dungeon and given into the custody of a jailer so crude, coarse, and uncouth that he had been known to steal milk

from blind kittens and eat peas off his knife.

This grim, grisly, gruff, glowering gloombag locked
Abu Ali in the deepest, dampest, darkest dungeon of
them all, with only a stool to sit on and a small slit
high up in the wall to let in the air.

He had no sooner done this dastardly deed, when
such a great commotion arose in the courtyard that it
even brought Silver Bud to the window of her room.

To her alarm, misgiving, forboding, and dismay, she
saw the wicked princes dismount from their caravans,
to be warmly greeted by Sulkpot Ben Nagnag.

Chapter the Twelfth

Which Explains How Abu Ali, Greatly Helped By Loyal Friends, Was Nearly Able to Win the Day

Y ou may well have wondered, *Gentle Reader,* how Silver Bud had fared during Abu Ali's absence, and I cannot paint a carefree picture for you; for she had remained in deep disgrace with her father, and had been confined to her own apartments. She was not even allowed her daily walk round the lily pond and back.

This did not lessen the tender regard she felt for Abu Ali. True, he *had* been gone a long time; but as absence (even of the most humdrum kind) makes the heart grow fonder, you can well imagine how intensely fond her heart had now become.

Her faith in Abu Ali had never faltered for a moment. The possibility of his failing in his task had never occurred to her. The mere idea would have struck her as ignoble.

Thus her first reaction to the noise in the courtyard was one of hope that Abu Ali had at last returned; but when she saw it was only the wicked princes, the joy vanished from her face, the sparkle faded from her eyes, and she turned away from the window, a prey to deep foreboding.

'Oh, dear!' she cried, and wrung her hands. 'What *can* have delayed Abu Ali? And *why* couldn't it have delayed the wicked princes instead? Oh, Abu Ali, hasten, hasten, or all is lost! Oh, *why* did I ever think of the tasks?'

What an appalling predicament yawned before her! Unless Abu Ali appeared within the hour, Sulkpot Ben Nagnag would wed her to whichever wicked prince had brought back the bigger carpet!

Little wonder that her eyes brimmed with tears and despair all but overwhelmed her!

All too soon, the door of her apartment was unlocked from the outside, and Sulkpot Ben Nagnag ushered in the wicked Princes Tintac Ping Foo and Rubdub Ben Thud.

They were carrying the magic carpet and the tail feathers between them, and looking as smug as ever.

'All hail to thee, fair Silver Bud!' smirked Rubdub. 'We return triumphant, as you can see! Here is the last magic carpet in the world! A priceless object, obtained only at the extremity of human endurance, super-human courage, and unbelievable tenacity!'

'This carpet flies like a bird!' crowed Tintac Ping Foo. 'You have only to step on it and state your destination (provided your weight is normal), and you're there in a flash!'

'And these,' cried Rubdub, 'are the magic tail feathers of the Phoenix bird! Examine them! Feel them! No deception! The only authentic tail feathers ever to be observed by mortal eye!'

'In short, daughter,' cried Sulkpot, radiating placid pleasure from every pore, 'your suitors have fulfilled Abu Ali's task as *well* as their own, to make up for the lack of a second carpet; therefore, the three of us have agreed that you shall choose between the carpet and the feathers without knowing which prince brought back which!'

'And may the best man win!' added Rubdub jovially.

'Well said, Thud!' said Ping Foo merrily. 'I knew you'd be a good loser!'

'Choose, child!' ordered Sulkpot.

'Never!' returned Silver Bud resolutely. 'I shall make no decision until Abu Ali returns!' and to show that the subject was now closed, she turned her back on them and walked to the other end of the room.

Ping Foo winked at Rubdub and then at Sulkpot, (who was in on it too), and then coughed.

'Dear lady. Alas. This gives me great pain,' he said in a very sorrowful voice. 'I regret to inform you that Abu Ali was eaten by dragons last Tuesday. We were there, Ben Thud and me, and saw it all.'

'R.I.P.,' said Rubdub, pretending to flick a tear from his eye.

'P.T.O.,' said Ping Foo.

'R.S.V.P.,' said Rubdub.

'M.Y.O.B.,' said Ping Foo.

'Indeed? Well, well! Too bad!' said Sulkpot insincerely. 'He was a fine figure of a lad!'

'We'll never see his like!' agreed Ping Foo.

'Even horrid little children loved him!' said Ben Thud.

'A kind word for everyone!' said Ping Foo.

'Still; life must go on!' said Sulkpot.

'Yes, yes!' said Rubdub. 'Laugh and the world laughs with you, snore and you sleep alone!'

'Which of us noble heroes do you fancy, ma'am?' asked Ping Foo; scrounching up his eyes bewitchingly.

'Neither!' said Silver Bud coldly.

'*What?*' exclaimed Tintac Ping Foo in pained surprise.

'And I don't believe you, either!' added Silver Bud. 'You're telling stories, and you have a nose like a hockey puck!'

'You are beside yourself!' cried Sulkpot hastily, for Ping Foo had clutched his nose protectively and gone very red. 'If this is how you treat the advances of these two very fine princes, you shall spend the rest of your days in the darkest dungeon! Come, gentlemen!' he added to the wicked princes, who were gazing at Silver Bud in amazement and reproach. 'We will go to lunch!

Don't attach too much importance to this trivial tantrum! She'll come to her senses soon enough!'

Without another word he stamped out with the wicked princes, banging the door behind him and locking it again.

Left alone, Silver Bud's courage failed her for the first time; for although she scorned Ping Foo's tale on the grounds that he hadn't been able to prove a word of it, there was no way of *dis*proving it either; and now she was facing the mournful prospect of spending the rest of her life locked up in a dungeon; for not even wild horses could ever force her to marry either one of the wicked princes.

Below in the dungeon, meanwhile, Abu Ali had at last given up trying to kick down the door, and was sitting on the stool wondering what he could use to dig a hole in the wall and thus escape, when suddenly the straw on the ground began to rustle, and the next moment the mouse popped her head out and said: '*Hist!*'

'Mouse!' cried Abu Ali delightedly. '*How* did you get *here*?'

'Boomalakka Wee and Omar Khayyam and I waited and waited, and at last we decided that things had gone awry. Which indeed they have!' she answered. 'So a mouse at Omar Khayyam's house was considerate enough to escort me here and introduce me to the local mice, who are *most* civil. They took me on a tour of the entire place, and this is no time to beat about the bush, Abu Ali; things are looking murky! The wicked princes are at lunch with Sulkpot, and I heard him tell them that he's going to boil you in oil later this afternoon, to remove all evidence!'

'Things, as you say,' agreed Abu Ali thoughtfully, 'indeed look murky!'

'The thing is to keep calm and cool and do nothing impulsive!' advised the mouse. 'Oh; by the way; Omar Khayyam sent you his best wishes and said if there's anything he can do, you only have to let him know. Pointless of him, I thought; but he meant well. Your three tail feathers arrived safely. They're up in Silver Bud's room at the moment, locked in with her. The magic carpet is there too.'

'Oh, *that* old thing,' said Abu Ali without particular interest, and then blinked and sat up. 'The magic carpet!' he cried in jubilation. 'Mouse! Go to Silver Bud, and tell her what has befallen me! Tell her to expect me as soon as I've escaped from here, and to have the magic carpet unrolled and ready in front of an open window!'

'But how can you possibly escape from *here*?' asked the mouse.

'I'll manage somehow! I have to!' said Abu Ali simply. 'Meanwhile, stay at her side and lend her your moral support!'

'I'd love to; but I can't be in two places at once,' the mouse protested. 'I promised to go back and tell Boomalakka Wee and Omar Khayyam what's happened!'

'No! Your place is at Silver Bud's side; she is now friendless and alone!' said Abu Ali. 'But wait! I have it! Ask Silver Bud to write Omar Khayyam a note, and have it delivered to him by one of the local mice!'

'I know just the mouse to do it!' the mouse approved.

'Then off you go!' said Abu Ali.

'Like a flash!' said the mouse. 'If you'll promise me not to be rash and reckless!'

'I promise!' said Abu Ali.

'I'm proud of you!' said the mouse emotionally, and burrowed down into the straw and disappeared.

Abu Ali hurried to the door and pressed his ear to the grating. Near by he could hear the jailer eating a turnip.

'Jailer!' he called. 'Hullo! jailer! A stone has just fallen out of the wall in my cell! Shall I put it back?'

'Oh?' came the jailer's voice from near by. 'How big is the stone?'

'It's as big as the hole,' answered Abu Ali.

'And how big is the hole?'

'I'm not sure!' replied Abu Ali. 'I haven't crawled through it yet! Shall I try?'

'No! Don't move till I get there!' shouted the jailer hurriedly.

There was loud jangling outside, and then a key rattled in the lock of the door.

Abu Ali picked up a large clay water jug and skipped behind the door. When it opened and the jailer came in, he brought the jug down on the jailer's head with all his might.

Now this would have worked wonders if the jailer hadn't been wearing a helmet; but the jailer *was*. He was wearing a big brass helmet with a spike on top, and when the jug burst with a loud bang and jammed his helmet down a few inches nearer his nose, he merely said: 'Wow!' and pushed it back again just in time to see Abu Ali dashing out of the door; whereupon he instantly gave pursuit, bellowing, 'Stop him! Stop him!'

Abu Ali ran as fast as he could, but the jailer was

close on his heels, and never stopped bellowing. Only a nose ahead, Abu Ali whizzed round a corner of the passage, only to find himself heading *straight* towards five sentries who had heard the bellowing and were heading *straight* towards him.

Abu Ali stopped dead in his tracks and looked back at the jailer, who gave a roar of triumph and pounced at him; but *just* as the jailer pounced, Abu Ali dived under his legs, and the jailer dived head-first into the sentries, and as the passage was not only narrow but dark, the jailer and the sentries had frightful trouble telling friend from foe.

This allowed Abu Ali to double back along the passage until he reached the stairs that led to the entrance hall.

He sprinted up them two at a time, and had *just* reached the top, when he met a *huge* contingent of guards on their way down to the dungeons to investigate the disturbance made by the jailer and the sentries; and when they saw Abu Ali, they yelled aloud and charged him at the double.

By now, the jailer and the sentries had disentangled themselves and reached the bottom of the stairs, so Abu Ali found himself trapped fore and aft. The jailer and the sentries and guards were about to converge on him, when he suddenly noticed a large brass lamp hanging from a chain above his head, and he leapt into the air and caught it.

By now the guards were half-way down the stairs and running too fast to stop, so you can guess what happened – they collided head on with the jailer and the sentries, who were half-way *up* the stairs, and down they all rolled to the bottom with a clashing and clanging that echoed all over the house.

Meanwhile Abu Ali, having scrambled hand-over-fist to the top of the lamp, seized the chain, and began to swing the lamp with his feet until it was sailing backwards and forwards much too fast for anyone in his right senses to try and stop it.

The dungeons *and* the stairs *and* the entrance hall now swarmed with sentries and guards; and though Abu Ali was safe for the moment, it was clear to the stupidest of them that he couldn't spend the rest of his life swinging to and fro on the lamp, so they stood and waited for him to exhaust himself.

Fortunately for Abu Ali, the lamp was now sailing through the air at such speed that, on the next upswing, he aimed himself carefully at the front door; and then, as he came swooshing over the heads of the guards on the downswing, he let go.

The wind whistled in his ears as he sailed through the air towards the front door; and by the happiest of coincidences, the wicked Princes Tintac Ping Foo and Rubdub Ben Thud chose that identical moment to come running in at the front door followed by Sulkpot Ben Nagnag.

Abu Ali's feet met Rubdub's tum, and Rubdub catapulted back into Tintac Ping Foo, who collapsed on top of Sulkpot Ben Nagnag, and Abu Ali was out of the house and half-way across the courtyard before they had even realized what had hit them. In fact, they had only *just* begun to realize what had hit them when they were buried beneath an avalanche of guards and sentries who hadn't noticed them in time, and this time the language was really unpardonable.

From the courtyard Abu Ali doubled round the corner of the house to where a creeper grew against the wall; and by the time the guards had disentangled themselves from Sulkpot and the wicked princes, he had scrambled half-way up it.

Silver Bud, having heard the din below, ran to the window and looked out; and when she saw Abu Ali climbing up towards her, she gave a little scream of excitement and tugged the magic carpet as near to the window as it would go.

'We must all keep calm and cool!' the mouse kept shrilling nervously. 'Calm and cool! Cool and calm!'

'The key! The key!' screamed Sulkpot's voice outside the door. 'I've lost the key! Break down the door, you blockheads! I shall choke or something! *Break it down*!'

Heavy blows at once began to shake the timber of the door.

'Hurry, Abu Ali! Hurry! They're breaking down the door!' called Silver Bud desperately, leaning out of the window till she nearly lost her balance.

'Come back! You'll fall!' screamed the mouse, clutching desperately at her slipper.

Silver Bud grasped Abu Ali's sleeve and pulled with all her might until he tumbled over the window into the room.

'Quick! On to the carpet!' he cried as the door began to splinter.

'Every man for himself!' encouraged the mouse, leaping on to the carpet behind Silver Bud and Abu Ali.

'To Peking in China, carpet!' shouted Abu Ali,

and just as the door fell in with a crash, the carpet gracefully rose in the air and sailed smoothly towards the window.

Oh, Reader, Gentle Reader! How can I bring myself to tell you? The window wasn't wide enough!

When the edges of the carpet touched the sides of the window, the carpet simply came to a halt and hung motionless in the air. The guards leaped up and caught it by the edges, and their combined weights easily brought it to the floor again.

Alas! Once more, poor Abu Ali was overpowered by superior force and dragged back down to the dungeon.

Once more poor Silver Bud, locked in her room, faced the awful fate of marriage to a wicked prince or a lifetime of imprisonment.

At last, it seemed, the wicked princes had triumphed.

Be that as it may, however, we must direct our attention elsewhere for a moment, for unknown to Abu Ali, other strange events were even now being set in motion.

Chapter the Twelve and a Halfth

Which Brings the Story to Its Close

I trust, *Gentle Reader, that you have not underestimated* the conscientious nature of the mouse.

As soon as she had left Abu Ali in his dungeon, she had run swiftly up the inside of the wall to Silver Bud and told her all. Silver Bud at once wrote a note to Omar Khayyam telling *him* all; and a chivalrous local mouse had set off to deliver it at break-neck speed.

Unfortunately, he had never been out of the house before. The wide world confused him; he lost his way; and ended up in a sinister quarter of the town, where he narrowly escaped death at the claws of a one-eyed mongoose, and was hit by a rotten orange. He then forgot the address of Omar Khayyam's house, and being unable to read or write, was only prevented from running all the way back home for fresh instructions by the fact that he was hopelessly lost. In his darkest hour, however, he stumbled upon an itinerant musk rat who spoke mouse as well as musk, and directed him correctly.

More dazed than downhearted, the local mouse arrived at Omar Khayyam's house and delivered the note, first to a lifelike portrait of Omar Khayyam's mother, and then to Boomalakka Wee.

Boomalakka Wee, mistaking the local mouse for a gentleman caller bearing some kind of worthless goodie for the mouse, reduced the situation to such a mishmash of inarticulate cross-purposes in his efforts to explain that the mouse was not receiving callers, that the local mouse nearly bit him on the toe out of sheer exasperation.

At this point, Omar Khayyam detected writing on the note, saw it was addressed to him, and opened it.

'Cease! Hold! Stay!' he cried, and read the note aloud to Boomalakka Wee.

'Abu Ali locked up in a dungeon!' cried Boomalakka Wee aghast.

'He may be boiling in that oil this vewy minute!' cried Omar Khayyam.

'We must save him!' cried Boomalakka Wee.

'Yes; but how?' asked Omar Khayyam.

Their quandary did not go unobserved, however; far away in the forest on the edge of the Arabian Desert, Nosi Parka the egg head was gazing intently into his crystal, feelingly following the fluctuations of the unfortunate fate that had befallen Silver Bud and Abu Ali.

Nosi, being calm and wise, did not fluster. He rose and went into the forest and gathered a pile of kindling.

Then he made a fire in front of his cave.

Then he fetched a blanket, and began to send up smoke signals.

To whom; Gentle Reader?

To whom else than the magician in the Land of Green Ginger?

It took an egg head to think of such a resourceful idea.

Meanwhile; back in the tent shop, Omar Khayyam

and Boomalakka Wee were pacing the floor and racking their brains to no avail. Every time they passed each other, they looked at each other hopefully, and then both shook their heads hopelessly and continued pacing.

At the place of execution at Sulkpot Ben Nagnag's house, the guards had begun to light the furnaces under the oil vats.

Locked in her room, Silver Bud lay sobbing on her couch; and the mouse, obeying to the letter Abu Ali's orders never to leave her for a moment, dabbed mimosa water on her sorrowing charge's forehead.

Downstairs, the wicked princes filled in the time before the execution by cheating Sulkpot at 'Button, button, who's got the button?'

In his solitary cell, Abu Ali sat and prepared himself for the worst, still determined never to admit defeat.

And then, somewhere at the back of his mind, a thought suddenly stirred.

He sat up straight and frowned with concentration.

The thought became wide awake.

The lamp!

What had Boomalakka Wee said? 'The spell only works for one person at a time . . . and as I can't get *back*, father can't get *here*!'

But since then, the spell had been *un*clogged by the magician! Boomalakka Wee *could* get back!

Abu Ali slapped his knees excitedly and leaped to his feet. All he had to do was send another message to Omar Khayyam, telling him first to send Boomalakka Wee home, and *then* to rub the lamp for Abdul, who would come roaring to the rescue!

Ah, but how to send the message? And was there still time, in any case?

Oh, how powerless he felt! So near, and yet so far!

At that crucial moment, there was a rap on the grille of his door, and when Abu Ali peered out, he found Kublai Snoo peering in from the other side.

'It's only me,' said Kublai Snoo shyly. 'The captain and I are just off for our camel ride. As you won't be here when we come back, I brought you a raisin bun and a banana.'

He passed them graciously through the grille.

'How very kind of you,' said Abu Ali, touched.

'And I'd like to take this opportunity to apologize to you for the regrettable incident of the hollyhock bed, Kublai Snoo.'

'Oh, please! Think nothing of it!' Kublai Snoo assured him. 'I think it's a shame they're going to boil you in oil! Do you have a farewell message? I'd be glad to forward it to your family!'

'Will you? How *doubly* kind of you!' exclaimed Abu Ali gratefully. 'My nearest kin is Omar Khayyam the tentmaker in the shop near the market place. Would you kindly go to him at once and tell him to send Boomalakka Wee back home, and then rub the lamp for Abdul? And would you repeat the message to me once, to make sure you have it right?'

'Tell Abdul to send Lakkawee home, and then Boom the Lamp for Omar Khayyam!' said Kublai Snoo obediently.

'Nearly, but not quite,' said Abu Ali patiently. '*Tell Omar Khayyam to send Boomalakka Wee back home, and then rub the lamp for Abdul!*'

'Wasn't that what I said?' asked Kublai Snoo in genuine surprise.

'Perhaps I'd better write it down,' offered Abu

'No, no, I'll remember it!' promised Kublai Snoo confidently. 'Besides here comes the captain to fetch me! I must fly! Ta-ta!'

He disappeared from the grille, leaving Abu Ali gravely doubting whether the message would reach Omar Khayyam at all, let alone in any condition to be of use.

Meanwhile, high in the air and far, far away, the Land of Green Ginger was sailing blithely through the sky towards the forest where Nosi Parka was sending up the smoke signals.

Unfortunately, just a *moment* before they came in sight of each other, there was a sudden downpour of rain.

The magician at once sailed the Land of Green Ginger over the top of the rainclouds; and the rain put out the fire that Nosi Parka had built.

Nosi Parka patiently waited for the rain to stop and the wood to dry, then began all over again.

In Omar Khayyam's tent shop, Omar Khayyam stopped pacing up and down.

'Anything's better than this infuriating inaction!' he announced to Boomalakka Wee. 'Let's go to Sulkpot's house and see what we can learn from the gatekeeper!

'Anything you say,' agreed Boomalakka Wee, 'is better than this whatever – you – said!'

So they set off swiftly for Sulkpot's house, leaving the lamp on the table of the tent shop and the local mouse in a deep sleep of sheer exhaustion in a hole in the wall of the spare bedroom.

As they crossed the market place, they passed Kublai Snoo and the captain, who were on *their* way to Omar Khayyam's tent shop, but of course nobody recognized anybody, never having met.

Meanwhile, the oil vats in the place of execution began to bubble and boil, and Sulkpot and the wicked princes were being shown to their front row seats.

It was shameful the way the wicked princes clapped and whistled when they saw a *huge* contingent of guards marching past on their way to fetch Abu Ali from the dungeon.

Up in Silver Bud's apartment, the mouse had run out of mimosa water, and was in a quandary.

Chancing to peer out of the window, she saw the *huge* contingent of guards marching towards the dungeons, and, guessing the worst, she hurled herself into the hole in the wall and almost *dived* the entire distance to Abu Ali's dungeon.

'Mouse, you're a mind-reader!' cried Abu Ali joyfully. 'I tried to send a message to Omar Khayyam to send Boomalakka Wee back home, and then rub the lamp for Abdul – but I'm *sure* it won't reach him in recognizable form!'

'Yes, it will! I'll go myself!' cried the mouse heroically. 'Meanwhile, use every trick you can think of, Abu Ali, to delay the boiling!'

She had no sooner vanished into the pile of hay than the cell door was unlocked and flung open, and in marched the *huge* contingent of guards.

They chained Abu Ali by the arms and then by the legs, and then chained the arm-chains to the leg-chains; and a particularly mean-spirited guard even went so far as to eat the raisin bun and the banana.

The mouse had barely scrambled through a hole in the garden wall on her perilous race to Omar Khayyam's tent shop, when Omar Khayyam and Boomalakka Wee arrived at the front gate of Sulkpot's house and banged loudly.

And Nosi Parka had just got his second fire going.

And high in the air; far, far away; the magician began to detect trouble with the steering of the Land of Green Ginger.

He hastened to his book of spells and began to check each one carefully; and the Land of Green Ginger began making such curious swerves that the lady

Phoenix bird lost her balance and toppled backwards off a branch into the stream, *insisting* to her husband as she fell that somebody had pushed her.

Meanwhile, the valiant mouse was dashing and skipping and darting through the crowded streets of Samarkand with a much better sense of direction than the local mouse; but even so, it was an exhausting ordeal for her, and only her steady, stalwart qualities kept her on her toes.

Things were worsening everywhere.

The gatekeeper remembered Omar Khayyam and Boomalakka Wee from the time he had admitted Abu Ali, so he opened wide the gate, pretending to be very hospitable and respectful; and as soon as they entered, he slammed it behind them and yelled for the guards; so now Omar Khayyam and Boomalakka Wee were prisoners too.

This piece of treacherous chicanery so enraged Boomalakka Wee that he stamped his foot in frustration; and having inadvertently used the right foot, he vanished forthwith into a green cloud, leaving the gatekeeper unnerved and Omar Khayyam twice as confused as he had been before.

Meanwhile, the Land of Green Ginger was flying over Nosi Parka's cave, and the magician just had time to read the smoke signals before he was swerved sharply off course again, due to circumstances beyond his control, though naturally the news of Abu Ali's predicament profoundly affected him.

At Sulkpot's house, Abu Ali was being marched to his place of execution, where the oil vats were now bubbling so ferociously that the reflected heat alone was being used for roasting chestnuts.

Meanwhile Kublai Snoo and the captain had found their way to Omar Khayyam's tent shop, and were banging on the door. They very soon tired of *that,* and the captain pushed it open and went in.

When they found there was nobody home, they were about to leave again when Kublai Snoo saw the lamp on the table and picked it up.

'Now *there's* a coincidence!' he exclaimed in delighted surprise.

'No, it isn't!' said the captain. 'It's just a dirty old lamp.'

'I know! My old grannie had a lamp *exactly* like this one, only not so dirty!' said Kublai Snoo sentimentally. 'My; it *is* dirty, isn't it? I'll just give it a quick polish!'

'No, we'll be late for our camel ride,' began the captain, but his voice was drowned in a terrible clap of thunder, and the floor split open *right* under their noses.

Kublai Snoo was so terrified that he leaped in the air and clutched the captain round the neck; but as the captain had leaped in the air and clutched *Kublai Snoo* round the neck in equal terror, they both fell to the floor with a crash as a huge green cloud rolled up into the room, and the awe-inspiring voice of Abdul boomed: 'I am the slave of the lamp! Ask what thou wilt and it shall be done!'

'Oh, please sir, don't eat us!' sobbed Kublai Snoo, quite undone. 'If you'll let us off this time, we promise never to do it again!'

'Do *what* again?' asked Abdul, mystified. You must have needed me, or you wouldn't have rubbed the lamp! What is your wish?'

'It's all a dreadful dream!' whimpered the captain. 'I knew I shouldn't have eaten such a heavy lunch!'

'What?' exclaimed Abdul incredulously. 'You called me all this way just to cure your *indigestion*?'

'No, no!' cried Kublai Snoo in a panic. 'We don't want to be cured of *anything*! We just want to get out of here while we're still in one piece! Oh, my goodness, I *wish* I'd never given that raisin bun and that banana to Abu Ali! I was *only* trying to be kind!'

'Abu Ali?' repeated Abdul swiftly. 'Where is he? Why didn't *he* rub the lamp? If he's in trouble, woe betide his enemies!'

'Well; *we're* not his enemies!' quavered Kublai Snoo. 'We don't even know him! And even if we *did* know him, we wouldn't harm a hair of his head; neither of us! *Please*, sir, can we go now?'

'Well, I suppose so,' said Abdul in perplexity, 'But I warn you! Don't try and summon me again after a false alarm like this! Because I have no intention of appearing!'

'No, no! Quite! Pray don't!' twittered Kublai Snoo. '*Good*-bye, sir; and *thank* you for not eating us!'

The highly offended Abdul began dissolving back into his cloud, and Kublai Snoo and the captain were just beginning to heave sighs of relief, when the mouse staggered out of a hole in the wall, more dead than alive.

'Stop! Wait! Come back!' she squeaked, the moment she saw Abdul.

'What? Again?' growled Abdul resentfully.

'*Eek! A mouse!*' cried the captain, leaping on to a chair.

'You *are* Abdul, aren't you?' cried the mouse urgently. 'Yes, you must be! I detect the family the family resemblance to Boomalakka Wee! Oh, kind sir; hurry to Sulkpot Ben Nagnag's house! They're about to boil Abu Ali in oil!'

Abdul, half green smoke and half very irritated djinn, eyed her coldly.

'First of all, I want to know whom I'm to believe, and whom I'm not to!' he said ominously. 'Which of you three is telling the truth?'

'I am!' cried Kublai Snoo.

'I am!' cried the captain.

'They are not! *I* am!' cried the mouse.

'Let him beware who exhausts my patience!' Abdul warned them sternly. 'And let him doubly beware who lies to me!'

'Oh, glory ducketts; please *hurry*!' cried the mouse desperately. 'They're going to boil him in oil!'

'Not until I'm satisfied it's not a wild goose chase!' decreed Abdul. 'I'll take you first, madam! Do you have your credentials with you? If so, kindly produce them!'

Meanwhile at Sulkpot Ben Nagnag's house, the hour of execution had begun to strike.

Abu Ali stood on a trap-door over the boiling oil vat, still chained and bound, and near by stood Omar Khayyam, also chained and bound, having been condemned to follow Abu Ali into the oil vat as an encore.

The wicked princes were sniggering all over their footling faces, and nudging each other, and flicking bits of rolled-up paper at the back of people's heads, and behaving exactly as one would expect spoilt and pampered brats to behave in public.

May I digress here for a moment to suggest to you, Gentle Reader, that the real test of a true hero is not how boldly he behaves when all is going well, but how nobly he behaves when all seems lost?

Suppose, for example, *you* were standing in chains, on a trap-door over a vat of boiling oil. Very few courses of conduct would be open to you; all of them unenviable. You could, perhaps, hammer your fists on your breast and lament your cruel fate; or you could unheroically grovel for mercy; or you could even defy your persecutors with scathing taunts. As a true hero, however, only *one* course would be open to you. You would have to rise above your tormentors, and show them how a truly brave man can die.

This was, of course, the course to which Abu Ali had decided to recourse.

Secretly, no doubt, he *might* have been reproaching himself for not having made use of his full royal title, no matter how unsporting it might have made the challenge. Secretly, no doubt, his heart *may* have been rending in twain at the thought of bidding farewell to Silver Bud, and all the joys and pleasures that should have been theirs to share.

Not a trace of it showed on his face.

What he *was* doing, in actual fact, was concentrating intently on Abdul.

'You *shall* get here in time!' he kept repeating to himself over and over. 'You *shall* get here in time!'

This I find quite admirable, Gentle Reader. The will to win is always half the battle. You are only as brave as you think you are. While hope is not lost, nothing is lost.

'Wretch! It is time to say your last words!' announced Sulkpot. 'Be brief and to the point!'

'Precisely *how* brief?' requested Abu Ali politely but formally. 'Can you give me the exact time at my disposal? It will obviously dictate my choice of subject matter.'

'I'll give you *exactly one minute*!' growled Sulkpot.

'I'm sorry,' replied Abu Ali regretfully, 'but if you'll try it yourself, you'll realize that one minute is insufficient time in which to compose a farewell address of any substance!'

'Nonsense!' shouted Ping Foo rudely. 'I could compose a *superb* farewell address in one minute!'

'So could I!' shouted Rubdub. '*Far* superberous!'

'Very well! Show me how!' invited Abu Ali courteously.

'Certainly!' cried Ping Foo, bouncing to his feet with delight at the idea of showing off. 'Ladies and Gentlemen! It is a far, far better farewell address I give you than anything old Rubdub Ben Thud would be able to compose! It is to a far, far better place I go than the place they'll send Rubdub! In the words of the dear old song: *I don't want to lose me, but I know I have to go –*'

'Time! Your minute's up!' shouted Rubdub disparagingly. 'And they were *pretty* feeble last words; weren't they, Sulkpot?'

'Hadly inspiring,' granted Sulkpot, vaguely beginning to wonder why the execution seemed to be getting out of hand.

'Then it's only fair to let Ben Thud do better!' insisted Abu Ali, nodding encouragingly to Rubdub.

'Prisoner! Be silent!' shouted Sulkpot at the same moment, having suddenly realized why the execution had got out of hand. 'You're just trying to play these two fine princes off against each other!'

'Sir, you wrong me!' objected Abu Ali with dignity. 'My sole concern is that Ben Thud should be given a fair hearing!'

'Hear, hear! Well said! Exactly!' cried Rubdub appreciatively. 'Ladies and Gentlemen of the jury –!'

'Speak your last words, prisoner!' interrupted Sulkpot fiercely. 'One minute from now, in you go, ready or not!'

'Very well,' said Abu Ali equitably. 'Then my last words are these, Sulkpot Ben Nagnag. If I were in your shoes, and one of these princes were about to become my son-in-law, I'd *much* prefer Rubdub Ben Thud!'

'Good heavens, why?' asked Sulkpot in amazement.

'Because he would steal far less of my wealth,' answered Abu Ali.

'Thank you, thank you; Abu Ali!' cried Rubdub, *immensely* flattered. 'Oh, how nobly said! I shall see you get a truly *beautiful* tombstone!'

'What will you inscribe on it?' inquired Abu Ali quickly. 'Nothing soppy, I hope?'

'No, no!' Rubdub assured him. 'Only the most heroic sentiments in the best blank verse!'

'I'll agree to it *only* if you promise me you'll compose them yourself!' said Abu Ali respectfully.

'Oh, I *will*!' promised Rubdub, preening. 'That's one thing I really excel at!'

'Sir,' one of the guards called to Sulkpot. 'The oil will soon be off the boil!'

'Then heat it up again, you blockhead!' cried Sulkpot.

'I would if I could, but we've run out of wood,' said the guard apologetically.

'Then boil him at once, ready or not!' bellowed Sulkpot. 'He's been playing for time, and we've been dolts enough to let him!'

'Release the trap-door!' shouted Sulkpot.

'Right!' called a guard, and pulled the lever. There was a loud and blood-curdling creak, and then something stuck.

'Oh, oh,' said the guard in embarrassment, 'it's stuck, boss! Won't be a jiffy!'

But as he began to tinker with the lever, a cry rang out.

'Who rang out that cry?' demanded Rubdub nervously.

'Me, Master! Look at that up there!' Small Slave yelled in terrified accents, pointing to the sky.

Everyone craned their necks upwards, and then a *wave* of alarm spread through the assembly.

Zooming down towards them like a great big wobbling wide-winged bird was the Land of Green Ginger.

Oh what chaos ensued! Oh, what panic and confusion! Everyone became as stupid as sheep and ran in the wrong direction at the same time; and the Land of Green Ginger had no sooner settled down on top of them all with a *Ker-Foomph, Ker-Woompha, Ker-Woomp!* when a huge cloud of green smoke rolled up out of the boiling oil vat, and Abdul's indignant face appeared in the middle of it.

'Everybody, except Abu Ali and Omar Khayyam, cease doing what you're doing; no matter what you're doing!' roared his angry voice; and *instantly* everybody except Abu Ali and Omar Khayyam was frozen into whatever undignified position they happened to be in at the time.

Abu Ali leap-frogged down from the trap-door, and as the magician came trotting through the ginger trees, hastily adjusting his spectacles, Abdul came to rest on the ground.

The mouse poked her head out of his sash, coughing slightly from the green smoke.

'Thank heaven, we're in time!' she cried, scrambling swiftly down his leg. 'And *however* did the Land of Green Ginger get here too?'

'Sheer coincidence!' called the magician proudly. 'It made its own way here, all by itself! My dear Abu Ali; what an *energetic* life you lead! Allow me to unchain you!'

'No, no! Allow *me!*' said Abdul, making a pass in the air with his hands. The chains at once fell from Abu Ali and Omar Khayyam with an obedient clatter.

'Silver Bud!' cried Abu Ali at once. 'I must tell her of our rescue! Which way is the house?'

'I'll consult my compass,' promised the magician; but

there was no need. At that very same moment Silver Bud came running towards them through the ginger trees.

'Abu Ali! I don't understand what's happened to our garden; but I'm *so* glad you're safe!' she cried in delight and relief, throwing herself into his open arms.

At this touching sight, the magician and Omar Khayyam and Abdul turned away discreetly and conversed with the mouse, allowing Abu Ali to dry Silver Bud's tears and kiss her lovingly on both cheeks and offer her a hundred other charming little attentions which are without importance except to those personally involved.

And all this time, Gentle Reader, Sulkpot and the wicked princes and the guards remained frozen into decorative ornaments – though I use the word decorative in its *loosest* sense. None of you, for instance, would win a prize if you had Rubdub Ben Thud crowding up your front hall with old newspapers tucked under his arm, an umbrella hanging from his nose, and galoshes piled up on his head. Besides which, his ridiculous expression of anguished alarm would upset your cat.

As for Tintac Ping Foo, his face was so furrowed with flabbergasted fear that even if you were to stand him out in the bean patch to scare birds, the puniest pewee would deride him with impunity.

Abu Ali now presented Silver Bud to Abdul and the magician, and as she had quite regained her composure, she greeted them charmingly, not forgetting to express her gratitude for the timeliness of their combined rescue.

'The only person I miss,' said Abu Ali regretfully 'And I *do* wish he was here, is Boomalakka Wee!'

'Me too,' confessed the mouse unexpectedly. 'I can't think why; but he *grows* on one!'

'Ho-hum!' said Abdul gravely. 'I'm afraid he's confined to quarters as a punishment for answering the lamp. However, I dare say he's learned his lesson!' He flicked his finger in the air, and Boomalakka Wee appeared in a puff of green smoke, looking as if butter wouldn't melt in his mouth.

Only the mouse detected that he was rubbing the seat of his green pantaloons rather tenderly, and she was too prim to call attention to it.

'But how,' she asked Abdul, when all the renewed welcoming had subsided, 'were you able to summon Boomalakka Wee, if only one of you can answer the lamp at the same time?'

'Come, come, little mouse,' said Abdul tolerantly, 'it is far too near the end of the story for long, complicated explanations!'

'Well, while there *is* still time, Abdul,' said the magician with the proper respect due a superior prestidigitator, 'I wonder if you would just look at the steering spell on my Land of Green Ginger? It appears to have developed an insoluble complication!'

'Certainly!' said the djinn. 'No doubt you need a touch more bat wing, or a touch less juice of poisonous mushroom,' and they wandered off into the ginger trees animatedly discussing the arts of incantation.

'Oh, dear, *look* at poor papa!' cried Silver Bud suddenly, noticing him for the first time. '*And* the wicked princes! *And* all the guards! Are they in pain?'

'No, no, my love,' Abu Ali consoled her. 'They're perfectly comfortable; and they'll only stay like that till we depart for Peking.'

'For Peking?' asked Silver Bud in understandable surprise. 'Why Peking?'

'Because,' said the mouse, bursting with pride at being the bearer of such impressive tidings, 'Abu Ali is none other than His Imperial Highness, Prince Abu Ali of China! Abdul told me!'

'My goodness!' exclaimed Omar Khayyam. 'He told me that himself; and I took it for a whopper!'

'*I* knew it all the time!' boasted Boomalakka Wee; which *was* only boasting; but he was so anxious to appear right about *something* for once that no one contradicted him.

'Why *ever* didn't you tell my father that?' Silver Bud asked Abu Ali in profound amazement. 'He wouldn't have *dared* boil you in oil!'

'No,' agreed Abu Ali. 'Nor send me on the task. But I mightn't have impressed you *half* as much, dear Silver Bud, if I'd just swaggered in here in my royal robes like any other prince, with everybody bowing and scraping to me!'

'For shame! You'd have impressed me *exactly* as you did, no matter *how* you'd come here!' Silver Bud reproved him.

Abu Ali was much too wise to press the matter further.

'I shall always agree with whatever you say, my love,' he replied tactfully. 'Besides, what's done is done, and no bones are broken. And we do at least possess three tail feathers from a magic Phoenix bird, which we could have obtained no other way!'

'We do indeed!' agreed Silver Bud contentedly. 'Even if we never find a practical use for them!'

'They would make a superlative nest,' hinted the

mouse acquisitively.

'Then, they're yours!' said Silver Bud generously, and pressed them into the mouse's delighted paws.

The magician and Abdul rejoined them.

'Just to show you how all of us overlook the most simple essentials in our concern with material success for its own sake,' said the magician light-heartedly, 'one of the weasel's whiskers in the steering spell had become slightly bent, and I had never thought to check anything so trivial as a whisker! Abdul saw the trouble in a trice! So where would you and your bride like to go, Abu Ali? You have but to say the word!'

'To the Imperial Palace in Peking, if you please!' said Abu Ali.

'Take your seats, and *away* we go!' cried the magician, and the very next moment the Land of Green Ginger lifted lightly off the house of Sulkpot Ben Nagnag and skimmed away into the wide blue yonder.

I will not detain you with a long description of the joyous welcome Silver Bud and Abu Ali received when they returned home. The celebrations and the fireworks were the most splendifferous in the history of Ancient China; and Abdul even relented sufficiently to turn the Widow Twankey back into the Widow Twankey. Her experience had the excellent effect of mellowing her nature; people found it impossible to think of her as the same woman; she was never without a smile and a word of cheer.

A little hardship is a great builder of character.

I need hardly assure you that Silver Bud made Abu Ali the most delightful of wives and later the most indispensable of empresses; and you will be glad to hear that the mouse took up permanent residence with them.

I dearly wish I could add that she was eventually reconciled with her friend who had run away to sea; but even in tales such as this, not *everything* can end happily. The fate of the friend remained an inscrutable equation, and *she* remained a spinster to the end of her long and rewarding life.

And that, patient and forbearing Reader (to whom it has been a pleasure to address myself) is the wonderful tale of the Land of Green Ginger.

A note about the edition you have just read:

This story was first published in 1937 with the longer title, *The Tale of the Land of Green Ginger,* and colour illustrations by Noel Langley himself. In 1964, Langley read the book for a New York radio station and this broadcast was so successful that the story was edited down to fit on an L.P. The edited version was published in 1966 with new illustrations by Edward Ardizzone. In 1975, the story was shortened once again, and it was this edition that stayed in print for the next forty years . . . until now.

The book in your hands contains the 1966 text, brought back by popular demand. This version has many fans, including the author Neil Gaiman, and it was these fans that persuaded the publisher to reissue this older, longer story. We hope that you have enjoyed it.

If you enjoyed

The Land of Green Ginger

why not read more
Faber Children's Classics . . .

→ FABER CLASSICS ←

T. S. ELIOT

Old Possum's Book of Practical

CATS

WALTER DE LA MARE

PEACOCK PIE

A Book of Rhymes

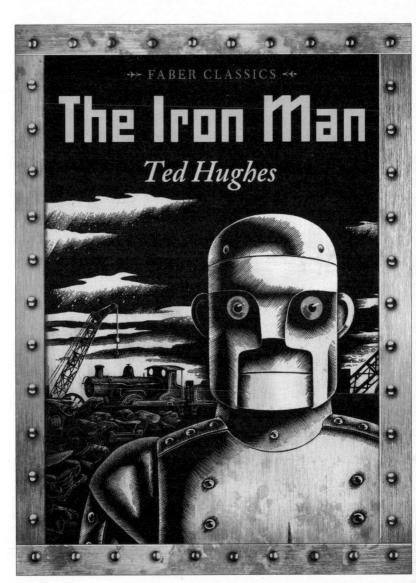

→ FABER CLASSICS ←

The Iron Woman

Ted Hughes

SYLVIA PLATH

The It-Doesn't-Matter Suit and other stories

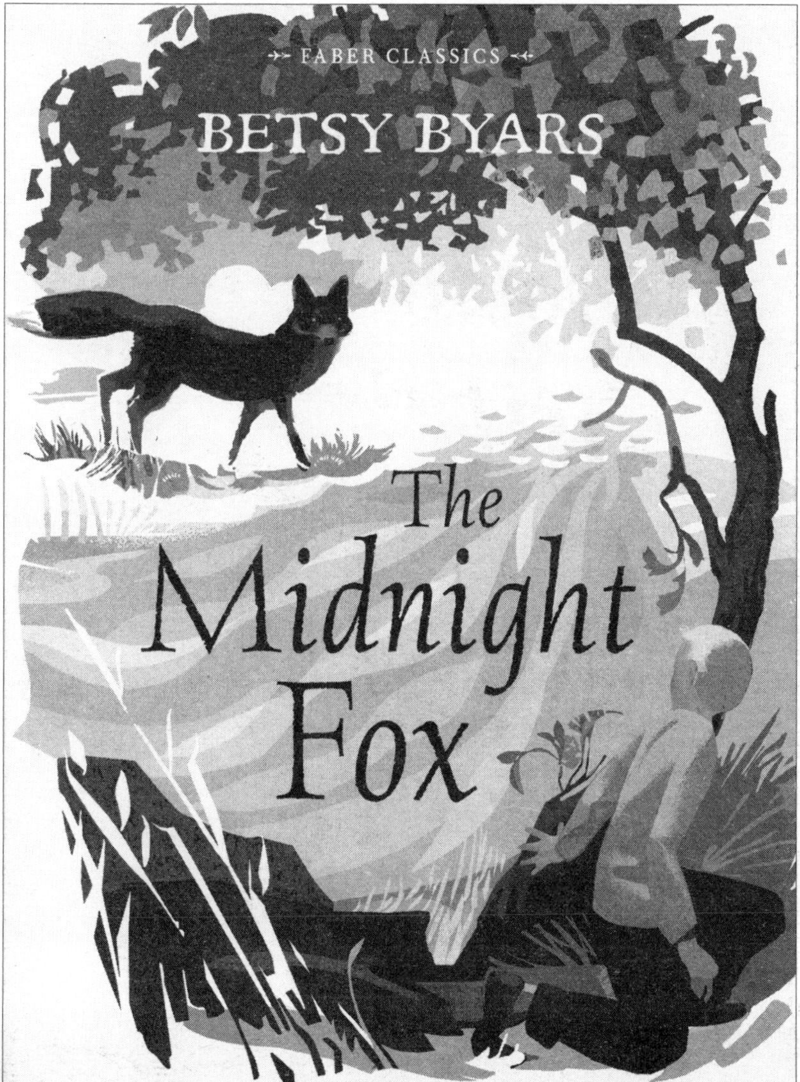
FABER CLASSICS
BETSY BYARS
The Midnight Fox

→ FABER CLASSICS ←

GENE KEMP

The Turbulent Term of Tyke Tiler

CARNEGIE
MEDAL
WINNER